ENTANGLEMENT *of* DECEIT

CHRIS BROOKES

A SCHNAUZER PUBLICATION

First published in 2016 by Schnauzer Publications

Design by Spiffing Covers Ltd

A CIP catalogue record for this title is available from the British Library.

All enquiries to: enquires@chrisbrookes.info

ABOUT THE AUTHOR

Chris lives in Sheffield, England with his wife and his two children.

After spending time in the army, he embarked on a career in musical theatre production and went on to co-produce touring shows in the 1980's. However, after discussions with his bank manager and the revelation that a mortgage needed to be paid monthly, it was agreed he would also seek a 'proper job'. Soon he found himself working in service delivery management, but all the while continued to pursue an interest in the stage, script writing and organising shows.

With his children starting to leave the nest, he decided the time was right to return to his creative roots and began writing full-time, developing the characters for an entangled mystery series based on the registers of a police court missionary. Originally intended for screen production, he wrote several scripts and began pitching the idea to television production companies. After very positive feedback from the BBC, he was also persuaded in 2012 to write the storylines as distinct novels. Then, in 2013, Schnauzer Publications released FATE, the first in the 'Entanglement' series of mysteries. Throughout 2014, Chris was busy writing the second book REVENGE, and in autumn 2016 the third book DECEIT was published.

Away from writing, Chris has always loved to sketch and, over the years, has produced numerous limited editions of his work. With more time now available, he hopes to once more pick up his pastels.

ACKNOWLEDGEMENTS

I am inspired by many people when writing. Sometimes it might be their personality that helps me develop a character, other times, it could simply be their music or a particular song that resonates and provides a scene or setting in my mind. To all the people who influence me, my heartfelt thanks.

When asked how I write, I reply "as if I am watching and describing a film." To build these raw images with words into a meaningful novel, however, requires a lot of development and editing. Enter my editor Helen Hancock, who quietly takes each chapter as I write it and helps turn it into acceptable prose. Helen's contribution to my novels is immeasurable – A sincere thank you, Miss Red Pen!

My gratitude goes to Claire Whiting for sharing the experiences of her son's autism, which helped me when developing the character of Daniel. Also, thanks to Amy Procter for her knowledge on the subject. I'm grateful to Brian Hyden and Lucy Tench for allowing me to tap into their historical knowledge and research expertise. It never ceases to amaze me where they manage to find, sometimes obscure, information in order to validate the facts I present.

As always I have to thank my small group of beta readers for giving up their time to read and offer feedback on my work prior to publication. Seldom do they shrink from giving me their blunt opinions, but I love working with them and find their comments invaluable.

Thanks to Spiffing covers for yet another great cover design in the book series. Also, my appreciation to Simon Parsons for his efforts in completing all the necessary formatting and ebook conversions of the 'Entanglement' novels.

Finally, my thanks go to my family and friends, who have always offered their encouragement for my writing career. However, nobody deserves more credit for this than my wife Kate, who unconditionally gives me her love and support in order that I can achieve my dreams.

Author's Note

In telling my story, I have drawn inspiration from what we know of the people and events of 1917. However, the details I have given of German espionage activities and the work of the intelligence services at that time are not necessarily taken from historical records. I would not wish this book to be seen as providing an accurate historical description of any specific WW1 spying or intelligence operations.

Chris Brookes

Chapter 1.

London, 1917

To an experienced porter who knew the peculiarities of every train that arrived on platform 3, something appeared different about the train pulling into St. Pancras Station. It wasn't the engine, sending a final billow of smoke high into the air towards the already blackened ironwork ceiling; nor the valve ports squeezing steam in all directions; nor even the high-pitched squealing from the huge wheels slowing to a stop. He couldn't quite put his finger on what it was, but something just felt wrong – the 1.40 into London seemed to have a sinister air about it.

The noise of carriage door windows opening broke his concentration. Hands of all shapes and sizes began reaching out for the brass handles. Then, like a swarm of ants leaving the nest, passengers began to spill out onto the platform. Within seconds, people bathed in uniform shafts of sunlight peppered with dust started to blend neatly into the frenzied activity of a capital city's railway station. That is, until a horrified scream from a distraught passenger twenty yards up the platform brought everyone to a sudden halt. The gasps that followed revealed exactly what was wrong.

With the train beginning to approach its top speed, the compartment door had slid open. Stepping inside, the attendant gave a pleasant smile and requested to see everyone's tickets – everyone being a woman on one side of the carriage and a well-groomed army chaplain on the other.

'Miss,' prompted the attendant. When there was no response, he repeated himself, this time slightly more assertively. Only then did the woman look up, with an expression suggesting that although she'd heard him, what he'd said hadn't really registered.

'Your ticket please, miss.'

'Oh yes, of course. I'm so sorry,' replied the woman with embarrassment. She opened and fumbled through her small purse. 'Ah! … There you go.'

The attendant checked the ticket's validity, punched it firmly, and handed it back to the woman, who gave a nervous smile before returning to her worried look, her eyes straining to see down the corridor. She glanced across to the chaplain opposite, and once more gave her anxious smile.

Having waited for the attendant to exit, the chaplain felt he had to mention his concern. Leaning forward, he very politely remarked in his soft and reassuring voice,

'Please excuse me, miss, but ever since entering the compartment, I couldn't help noticing the worried look on your face. Is everything alright?'

He'd used the word 'miss' more out of habit than astuteness. The woman was clearly wearing two rings on her wedding finger.

Did her fear really show that much, she wondered, briefly catching a glimpse of her reflection in the window. In truth, her look was one of tense anticipation rather than genuine fear. 'I'm fine —,' but she paused, realising that she wasn't sure how to address an army chaplain.

Luckily he sensed as much. 'Just "chaplain" is usual,' he smiled.

Giving a coy shrug of her shoulders, she promptly got to her feet and gathered up her coat. 'If you read about something awful in tomorrow's papers, chaplain, please do say a prayer, won't you?'

It was such a strange thing to say; and before the chaplain could even attempt a reply, the woman had left. He watched as she walked briskly along the corridor, constantly checking behind herself.

Quickening her pace, the woman felt her lip quiver nervously. Tiny beads of sweat began to break through the powder on her forehead. Seeing the countryside beyond the window rush past her head made her feel dizzy and disorientated. A sudden hollow booming, followed by the deafening clatter of a passing train startled her and brought back her focus. Again she checked behind herself. Her breath became short gasps.

Somebody was there, she knew it.

As the final carriage of the passing train disappeared into the distance, the noise in the corridor returned to normal – although she began to realise that normal wasn't the squeal of a bulb being slowly unscrewed from its holder.

'Who's there?' she stuttered, naïve enough to expect an answer.

A final turn of the bulb was perfectly timed with the train entering a tunnel. The corridor was immediately plunged into total darkness.

There was no scream, but these things were always efficiently done.

~~~

The station porter's request for passengers to move away had been authoritative enough, but still they chose to ignore him and continued to gawp at the terrible scene. Only when the police arrived could the whole area be sectioned off, so that investigations could begin in earnest. People were finally ushered away from the gore which lay in front of them – a body caught in the couplings of two carriages and
~~~

so badly mangled in places that it was hardly recognisable as a human being. A filthy and badly torn dress gave a clue that the body was female; that, and a helpless dangling hand which had two rings on the third finger.

'Come along now, sir, move along,' called out the porter, holding out his arms to guide the man away.

'I was thinking I might be of some use,' offered the man, pushing back a thick lock of blond hair. 'I'm a surgeon you see.'

The porter glanced back towards the carnage. 'I think she needs more than a surgeon, sir.' Deciding the man appeared genuine, he dropped his arm and allowed him to pass through the cordon.

Once up close, and watching two police constables slowly untangle the body and lay it on the platform, it was obvious what the porter had meant. Giving the men a nod he introduced himself: 'Tom Sharpe. I'm a surgeon at St Thomas's. I was going to offer my help but I can see now there's no point.'

Tom had been at the station waiting to catch his train home when, in all the commotion of an emergency, he felt compelled to offer medical help. Seeing one of the constables cover his mouth and retch, Tom gave an understanding smile. 'Not pleasant is it? Look, I'm used to seeing this sort of thing. Let me deal with the body until the ambulance arrives. You chaps go and help keep people away.

There wasn't much objection.

Alone with the corpse, it was only a matter of time before Tom wanted to inspect the body in an attempt to find out the cause of death. Ten seconds was the best he could manage before he started muttering, 'No gunshot wounds … or stab marks. Totally obliterated face … massive trauma to the neck … huge blood loss … evidence of cerebrospinal fluid …. He turned the body slightly. 'Burning to the arms – likely not intentional. Umm!'

A voice broke his concentration. 'Well, if I'd known the revered Professor Sharpe was in attendance I wouldn't have rushed.' Tom knew instantly whose jovial sarcasm it was – Dr William Goddard from the coroner's office.

'William!' Tom greeted him and stood up to offer a handshake. He could see from the look on the doctor's face that he needed to give an explanation as to why he was here. With clarification done, the pair were soon in light-hearted conversation, which to a bystander, could seem cold and heartless, given they were talking over a mutilated body, although, for two medical men used to dealing with terrible traumas on a daily basis, this was quite normal.

'Go on then, what's the cause of death? Was it murder or an accident?' Dr Goddard joked.

'Oh, I'll leave that one to you boys to decide.'

'What, not even a theory from you, Tom?' the doctor teased, screwing up one eye and inclining his head to one side playfully.

Tom laughed. 'Not really. The burning to the arms is interesting though.'

The doctor waved his finger and beckoned Tom to join him down by the body. 'When it's suspicious, I start with the finger nails.' He winked and picked up the dead woman's hand. 'Invariably tells me if there was a struggle or if she desperately tried clinging to something.'

Giving a smirk in recognition, Tom took the hand from the doctor and proceeded to inspect the nails. Suddenly he froze in shock and went pale, a massive adrenaline rush hitting his stomach and groin. With dread he slowly turned the wrist of the hand to fully show the back of it. He just stared. 'No, God, please, it can't be,' he muttered.

But it was! Tom was looking at Mary's engagement and wedding rings.

'No … no … please, no!' he shouted.

'Tom, what on earth is it?'

Tom didn't answer. Blind panic was setting in. He cradled the back of the woman's head and brushed away the filthy dark and badly singed hair from her dreadfully damaged face. He searched desperately for a sign it was Mary; but there was too much destruction; he just couldn't tell. 'Scar,' he yelled, gaining a rush of logic. The only way he'd know for sure, was if he saw the scar from the operation she'd had two years earlier. He began to rip away at the layers of her clothing.

'Tom! … Stop! Good god man, what's wrong with you. Stop it.'

But Tom heard nothing, other than his inner voice telling him to keep hoping – to cling to the possibility this wasn't his wife hanging pitifully in his arms. He clawed desperately at the corset, but couldn't rip it open. Dr Goddard's solid hands swiftly took hold of Tom's shoulders and pulled him away.

'Are you mad? Whatever is it? Tell me!'

Struggling frantically, Tom yelled, 'The scar, I've got to see the scar.'

It made no sense to the doctor. Whatever had happened to make Tom suddenly go berserk?

'I have to know!'

'Know what?'

Tom tried another lunge forward to try and free himself, but one of the police constables had now returned and was able to help the doctor hold him down. Trembling with a combination of fear and anger, he finally gave up the struggle and began to weep in desperation.

'It's Mary, William … it's Mary!'

Chapter 2

One month earlier – Sheffield

Elliott breezed into the police station with his usual exuberance, but got no more than three paces towards the counter before the strong smell of raw onion and garlic started attacking his senses. The court missionary could cope with most smells – but onion was certainly not one of them. As for garlic, to Elliott, the mere use of the word should have been made a criminal offence. Peering over the counter he quickly saw the culprits stuck on forks and standing upright in a jar. His expression took on a deep snarl of disapproval.

'I know! Stinks like 'ell, dunt it, Mr Elliott,' remarked the young constable whilst making his way over to the counter. 'Sergeant Drake's idea. Reckons it'll ward off all these colds going about.'

Elliott tried hard to alter his look of dissatisfaction to something resembling acceptance, but his nostrils didn't want to play along. 'Think it might also strip some varnish off this desk in the process,' he grimaced. 'Is the inventive sergeant about?'

The constable gave a smile and duly went in search of his superior, who arrived in due course, sporting a smug look – not for implementing an old wives' tale, but for something far more intriguing, and a tale he was bursting to tell. Smugness towards Elliott on Drake's part usually meant he was holding an offender whose detention would cause scandal and embarrassment for the middle classes. In this case, it was a man who had been followed underneath a canal bridge and unceremoniously arrested once in the act of making love to a young woman.

Thumbing down the register, Elliott did a double take at the entry for cell number 4. Had he read it correctly? 'You are joking!' he said with incredulity.

Drake gave a Cheshire cat smile, the pointed ends of his thick handlebar moustache rising to almost touch his eyelids. This was scandal of the highest order and he relished seeing Elliott's utter surprise. 'Nope! Just as it says, Mr Elliott: Judge Joseph Sanderson, charged with lewd, indecent acts in public.'

Of all the people Elliott could have imagined being detained in the cells, the judge would not have been even a possibility; and yet now here he was, a man he knew well and certainly respected within the judicial system. It all seemed unreal. Surely there must be a rational explanation. He turned to Drake, who was still showing a cloying smile at his prize catch.

'And there's no misunderstanding, no mistake, sergeant?' But Elliott knew that Drake didn't make such mistakes and particularly with a judge. He would have to have been 200 per cent sure that all facts were correct before he charged him.

'How even the mighty can fall,' Drake gloated.

Drake's self-assurance was beginning to irritate Elliott. He decided the sergeant needed reminding of a proverb or two: 'A clear conscience is usually the sign of a bad memory, Sergeant Drake. No matter what the judge may have done, at least temper your quest for justice with some mercy.'

It did the trick.

Walking into the cell, Elliott felt for the plight of the judge, sitting on the solitary bench with his head bowed.

'Judge Sanderson,' Elliott acknowledged, but the judge didn't lift his head to greet his visitor. The shame of his situation was almost too much to bear, Elliott surmised. Certainly it was totally out of character. In the eight years that the two men had worked together in the assize courts, the judge had been a most outstanding Christian and moral man. That he should be found in the city centre having sex with a woman, assumedly a prostitute, beggared belief. But after having dealt with the mess caused by a former friend, Canon Brockwell, and his perverse vices, nothing could really shock Elliott any more. What it did do, however, was chip away further at his faith in middle class morality.

Normally Elliott would have had an idea of how he should tackle the situation and question a prisoner, but this was new territory. He took a moment to gather his thoughts. Despite the culprit's identity, he realised that, ultimately, his assessment to a court would still have to present the facts and, although potentially embarrassing for both men, Elliott would have to learn the whole truth of the night's events.

He cleared his throat. 'Judge, you know I have no option but to ask you about last night. I will be required to give an opinion on the situation. However, if it is troubling for you to talk to me, I will request that I am removed from the case.'

At the very least, Elliott expected the judge to glance up and acknowledge his presence. But there was nothing. It was pathetic to see a once-fine individual driven to a depth of shame where he couldn't face looking at a colleague.

'I appreciate the difficulty in all of this, but —'. He stopped himself as something dawned on him. The judge was beginning to slouch more and more. Elliott became angry at his own stupidity. He was talking to someone who was fast asleep!

'JUDGE!' he bellowed, and at such a volume that he felt the word reverberate right through the station.

But the assumption that Judge Sanderson was asleep quickly turned to something far more disturbing. Elliott reached out his hand to touch the judge's shoulder, only for the large frame of the prisoner to topple over like a stunned animal at the slaughter house. Elliott knelt on the floor by the body and felt for a pulse at the neck, but the firmness of the flesh told him there wouldn't be one. The judge was clearly dead.

~~~

After nearly twenty years of marriage, Ann knew exactly what type of day her husband had had. A good, positive day would be indicated by him eating his dinner heartily, followed by eager conversation and interest in the boys; a less positive day would see him picking at his food and then wanting to read his newspaper and be absorbed in his music; a bad day would mean only the odd mouthful of dinner, accompanied by moans and groans about trivial things; and a really awful day would leave him sitting in silence, puffing furiously at his pipe and oblivious to the world around him.

Having only picked at his food, Elliott slumped down into his chair and took out his tobacco pouch. Oh dear, thought Ann, a bad and an awful day!

In an attempt to ensure her husband didn't sink into
~~~

excessive rumination over the obvious problems of his day, she decided to tease him. 'None of the wonderful Mr Gilbert and the delightful Mr Sullivan tonight, dear?'

Elliott was having none of it and gave his 'not amused' expression. There was a brief silence before he unexpectedly rattled out a question. 'What makes a successful, intelligent and highly regarded member of the judiciary risk everything for a quick bit of sordid gratification?'

'The desire for more of it?' Ann joked, unable to resist.

Elliott drew his eyebrows together in disapproval. His wife didn't have a clue what her husband was talking about. As usual, he had started a conversation in the middle of his thought process and just expected her to get the gist of it.

'Robert, dear, as much as you may think differently, I am not a mind reader. I haven't got the slightest idea what this is all about. You'll need to explain.'

Elliott fumbled at patting the tobacco deeper into the bowl of his pipe before striking a match. Speaking like a jumping record, he intermittently forced out his words as he drew in the smoke. 'You remember … Jo … seph … Sand …erson?'

'What, Judge Sanderson?' Ann asked, never being able to remember his first name.

'Yes,' confirmed Elliott and then began describing the

Elliott felt an obligation to visit the house of the judge a few days after the news of his death had broken. He wanted to offer any help he could with making arrangements for the immediate care of the son, although, having not seen the lad for over five years, he was unsure what he'd find. A stroll along Abbey Lane brought him to the judge's beautiful property, set well back from the road. He paused briefly at the bottom of the drive, taking a deep breath in anticipation. Arriving at the sandstone architrave that framed the entrance, it took several pulls on the bell cord before the door opened and Elliott was greeted by Mrs Sowerby. He was pleased to see she was alone.

'You're very prompt, Mr Elliott,' declared the housekeeper, with tear-filled eyes.

Elliott smiled. 'Habit of a lifetime.'

'Do please come in. I was just about to —' but she couldn't finish her words, and had to clasp her hand to her mouth to choke back her tears. She was clearly still shocked at the news.

Elliott was never really comfortable dealing with emotional situations. 'Would you like a little time alone before we speak, Mrs Sowerby?' was the best he could offer in terms of comfort.

Managing to gather her composure, the housekeeper explained that she was just about to make some tea and offered him a seat in a large formal reception room.

Elliott, however, thought they would probably feel more at ease chatting in the kitchen. Quickly agreeing, Mrs Sowerby led the way.

In mid conversation, when Elliott thought he had cleverly disguised the reason for the judge being in the police station, Mrs Sowerby interrupted. 'News of indiscretions usually travels fast, Mr Elliott. I am aware of the judge's … shall we say, most recent requirements.'

Quite surprised, and annoyed at the obvious leak of information from the police station, Elliott acknowledged the facts to the housekeeper with a polite, yet plainly forced smile.

'And how has Daniel taken it all?' Elliott asked, wishing to change the subject.

Closing her eyes and leaning her head back, Mrs Sowerby allowed herself a large and audible intake of breath. Looking at Elliott with some guilt she stated, 'He doesn't even know his father is dead yet.'

'I see,' replied a shocked Elliott, but he didn't see. Not until Mrs Sowerby explained.

'I know Daniel like he's my own. I have to choose the right time to tell him. It's better if he sees a lot of people visiting and then begins to ask me questions. Then I can lead him gently into events. He's used to his father staying away for a few days at a time, so right now things are normal. I beg you, will you let me just keep him in his little world of routine a while longer?'

Elliott smiled acceptingly. Who was he, he thought, to decide when the time was right to shatter someone's world.

Pouring out the tea, Mrs Sowerby turned her attention to practicalities. What would happen now? When would the funeral be? What preparations should she make? Unfortunately, Elliott didn't have many answers, but he explained as much as he was able.

'We need to first contact any immediate family. Perhaps you could find me some addresses or telephone numbers.'

'I'm not altogether sure he has any family, Mr Elliott: none that I've ever come across, at any rate.'

Elliott was beginning to realise that things might not be as straightforward as he had first envisaged.

The housekeeper placed her cup gently on the saucer. 'I know my future is uncertain, but what will happen to Daniel? If he has to go into one of those horrible places, it'll surely kill him.'

What neither of them saw was Daniel standing listening just outside the door; and for a boy whose condition meant he had a tendency to take things literally, this was devastating news. He fled petrified to his room. Once inside, he rocked himself and tapped his head continuously. After five minutes he stopped. The trigger was General Custer – he was out of place! Soon, Daniel was back immersed in his world of the US 7th

Calvary, repeatedly lining up his tin soldiers in precise little rows. Only the small wet patch on the ottoman gave any clue to his crisis.

That evening, after dinner, Daniel seemed in cheerful mood. His earlier experience, like any other which caused him anxiety, had been locked away in the recesses of his mind – where it posed no danger, and didn't have to be dealt with. As was the routine, he fetched the pack of cards, and counted them out carefully into two piles on the table. His face showed fierce anticipation at Mrs Sowerby's words, 'You first.' After only a few turns of the cards, his eyebrows began lifting cautiously as each subsequent one was laid down. Twelve cards in and his excitement exploded, 'Snap!' Mrs Sowerby smiled and gave her applause. She knew tonight was the right time to start preparing Daniel as best she could for a very different future.

'After the next game, Daniel, I want to talk to you about your father,' she began.

Chapter 3

No sooner had Elliott sat down in his chair and taken out his tobacco pouch than Lily, the housemaid, gave a discreet knock on the parlour door and entered.

Somewhat preoccupied with wiping the blood off her hands after gutting several mackerel in the kitchen, she said innocently, 'I forgot to tell you, Mr Elliott. A lady called on you earlier. I dealt with her appropriately but —'

'So we can see!' interjected Ann laughingly, but, from the confused look on Lily's face, it was obvious the joke was wasted. Ann didn't have the enthusiasm to explain, so instead, she smiled pleasantly and offered, 'Sorry, you were going to say, Lily.'

'Only that the lady has returned and is now at the door.'

Ann very much wanted to make another quip, but a shake of Elliott's head told her not to tease any further. He stood up and led the maid out of the room. 'All right, Lily. Thank you. I'll attend to things from here.'

It was with some surprise that Elliott opened the front door to Mrs Sowerby, accompanied by Daniel.

'I'm really sorry to disturb you at home, Mr Elliott, but I was hoping to have a chat with you before tomorrow,' stated the woman, who was clutching anxiously at an envelope.

Elliott never cared for dealing with things on the doorstep, and therefore immediately invited the pair inside. The obvious distress on the woman's face told him that the problem was serious enough to warrant traveling several miles to visit him. Once in the hallway he led the way to his study, stopping briefly to introduce the visitors to his wife.

'I hope you don't mind the intrusion, Mrs Elliott,' apologised Mrs Sowerby again. Like her husband, Ann could sense the woman's anxiety, and she also couldn't help but observe Daniel's unease, although in his case the nervousness was due to being out of his familiar environment. The practice of visiting people was clearly alien to him and therefore disconcerting.

'Listen, why don't you take a seat here in the parlour and discuss things? I'm sure you'll be more comfortable than in the study. Let me take your coats and I'll get Lily to make some tea,' offered Ann, her words drawing an appreciative look from Mrs Sowerby.

'And this must be Daniel. Mr Elliott has told me all about you, young man,' Ann continued, attempting to engage the attention of the boy, who was now trying to move behind his nurse and out of sight. He finally cast his eyes downwards like a small worried infant.

Elliott enquired, carefully, 'You have ... well, broken

the news of …?'

A nod of her head indicated the answer.

'And everything went —'

'As I expected it would,' interjected Mrs Sowerby.

'Expected it would' actually meant that Daniel hadn't given any instant reaction of grief to his father's death. Instead, he simply showed curiosity as to how he'd died, but without much emotion. Within ten minutes, the information had been assimilated and he was once more playing with his soldiers. It wasn't that he was uncaring or hard, merely that this was how his condition made him. Mrs Sowerby knew, however, that a reaction to the whole experience was likely to follow in a disturbing form at some stage in the future.

'Would Daniel like to play with our son, Cecil, while you chat with my husband?' asked Ann, unaware of the full extent of the boy's lack of interactional skills.

Not wanting to appear ungrateful, Mrs Sowerby gave a half smile. 'We could try,' she answered, knowing that Daniel's idea of play would prove anything but normal to Ann's son. With the introductions done, she eventually persuaded Daniel to follow Cecil to his room. Her instinct proved right when Daniel entered into a conversation with Cecil about engines, something he had no knowledge of.

'Yes, and General Custer has a bright red engine,'

Daniel excitedly explained.

Cecil just gave him a disparaging look.

Downstairs, Mrs Sowerby got to the point of her visit and handed Elliott the envelope she had been clutching, asking him to read the contents. It was a letter from a firm of solicitors based in Wales.

Flipping over the sheet of vellum paper and studying the text again, Elliott sighed in exasperation at the blunt tone of the letter. His opinion wasn't long coming: 'The prospect of obtaining money. There's nothing more likely to get low life crawling out of the woodwork!'

Mrs Sowerby shrugged and dropped her shoulders in a way that signalled defeat.

'No! Don't give in. This is nothing but flowery legal language,' snapped Elliott, waving the letter angrily. 'You leave it with me. I know a man who should be able to help. In fact, let me just check something,' he said, before storming off towards his study.

'I really didn't mean to trouble him ...' started Mrs Sowerby, directing her comments to Ann.

'Don't you worry, dear! My husband has to have a project, and I think whatever that letter contains might be his latest one.' She then smiled in resignation, 'I had hoped it might be felling the overgrown tree in the garden ... but hey ho!'

'Oh dear! I am sorry.'

With Elliott away busily sifting through some papers on his desk, Mrs Sowerby explained the situation, although there wasn't really a great deal to tell. It was simply a case of Daniel's mother resurfacing from wherever she had been and wanting to claim her estranged son. Of course, it was likely nothing more than a stunt for the mother to get involved and try to have some say in the management of her son's anticipated and sizable inheritance. In the view of her solicitors, there was validity in her argument that 'she was quite happy with Daniel's care whilst his father was alive. However, with that safeguard now having been removed, as his mother, she naturally wishes to assume responsibility for Daniel. The fact that she had made no contact over the years was conveniently ignored, as was the fact that Mrs Sowerby was, and always had been, Daniel's primary carer. The awful truth was that the housekeeper's care was classed merely as that of a domestic servant whose duties were no longer required. As for Daniel, until the position could be finalised, the intention was that his mother could provide all necessary care. Mrs Sowerby had little doubt that, in reality, this 'care' would result in a move to institutionalize Daniel.

'That's awful!' exclaimed Ann, aghast. She moved to sit by the visibly distraught Mrs Sowerby. 'Whatever help my husband can give, you must take it,' she insisted, clasping her own hands over the woman's.

'I can cope with my fate. That will be what it must be. But Daniel, he needs proper care, Mrs Elliott.'

'I know,' Ann softly reassured her.

Perhaps now wasn't the best time for the two young boys to re-appear in the parlour. Cecil was flustered and stomped to a halt. 'Is he stupid or something? Tell him, mother, that General Custer could not have had a red Wolsey or any other car for that matter!'

Poor Cecil, who knew nothing of mental illness, was quickly frog-marched out into the hall, where his mother firstly gave him a swift lesson on manners, and then attempted to describe what she knew of Daniel's condition.

~~~

'Well?' Elliott impatiently asked the man seated opposite him at the large desk.

'That's what I like about you, Robert, you conveniently forget that my business is about working for clients who pay for services rendered.'

'A mere triviality,' Elliott joked, and smiled apologetically at his friend and philanthropic solicitor, Ernest Cooper.

The solicitor placed the letter down on his desk and sat back. 'Very well,' he sighed, 'If I can help you with things, I will. But first, we need to establish who exactly the
~~~

executor of the estate is. If, as you say, Judge Sanderson has no family, I suspect he would have appointed someone legal. I'll make some enquiries.'

The next ten minutes were spent trying to hammer out some form of strategy. Invariably this meant Elliott taking an antagonistic approach to provoke a reaction. Cooper, however, needed time to think about things more carefully, although his initial reaction favoured a subtle approach, one that could effectively stall things. He knew that only once the will had been read could a proper game plan be implemented through probate.

'Right now, I feel we need to show that Mrs Sowerby is still needed. We have to be able to demonstrate to a court that her dismissal ought to be delayed, for the boy's sake,' Cooper commented, trying to push back in his chair enough to release the pressure of the desk on his oversized stomach. 'Perhaps a break would do it?'

'A break ...' mused Elliott, watching the desk inch closer to him.

'Yes, we'll argue that the judge had already planned a stay somewhere for Daniel – obviously with Mrs Sowerby going along. In the interests of all concerned, I think a court would agree that such a break could still go ahead.'

Impressed with his friend's tactics, Elliott sought reassurance. 'And that buys us some time?'

'Exactly ... So, all that's needed now is for you to

organise somewhere, Robert.'

'Oh, thanks,' frowned Elliott, but already he was playing with an idea. The trouble was, the people involved would need some convincing!

Chapter 4

The ever-increasing number of soldiers returning from France requiring surgery meant Tom Sharpe was now dividing his time between the King George Military Hospital and his own theatres at St Thomas's. It was at the former that he met the brilliant and pioneering young facial reconstruction surgeon, Major Richard Raven. The pair immediately struck up a friendship when Tom was asked to help the major with a convoy of severely wounded repatriated troops. Despite already working exceptionally long hours to complete his own daily list of operations, he willingly worked even longer to assist the major. However, working with Raven wasn't without its problems. In simple terms, Tom's role as a surgeon was invariably about destruction through amputation. Now, suddenly, he was subject to a totally different surgical discipline.

Tom pushed back the unruly locks of hair and cursed for the umpteenth time. No matter what cream or oil he used, these days it never seemed to keep his hair plastered down for long.

'Professor Sharpe,' came a gentle voice.

Tom gave a muted sigh of exasperation as, yet again,

his hair fell down over his eyes, but he turned to the nurse with an encouraging smile. 'Yes nurse.'

'I'm really sorry to bother you, professor, but I'm to ask you —'

Tom interrupted and playfully replied, much to the nurse's surprise, 'I'll answer your question, nurse, if you'll first answer mine.'

'Erm … well, yes, if I can,' replied the girl hesitantly.

'Do you have a sweetheart?'

The young girl immediately blushed and looked away. Having only been on theatre duties for two days, this was the first time she had witnessed Tom's eccentric behaviour – his way of maintaining some sort of sanity in all the insanity that surrounded him. Naturally she took his question as an inappropriate advance but, respecting his position, answered. 'Well, yes I do actually, but I will say —'

Again Tom interrupted. 'Excellent! Then tell me, nurse, exactly what does he use on his hair to keep it held down all day long?'

The poor girl was dumbfounded. 'Erm … well … I don't —'

Tom interrupted for the final time. 'Perhaps you would ask him and let me know.' He offered her an infectious smile. 'Right, what was it you were going to ask me?'

Giving another 'Erm,' she realised that she'd almost

forgotten why she did want him. Eventually she stated, 'Major Raven has sent me to ask you not to forget your three o'clock appointment.'

By the look on Tom's face and the raising of his brow, she thought the reply might be a bizarre one.

'Ah yes, thank you nurse.' He then looked her straight in the eye and said with a deadpan expression, 'At three o'clock the major and I will be dancing an "excuse me" with matron on the roof garden.'

As Tom strolled off, the bewildered nurse was left wondering if he was actually joking. A junior doctor and Tom's assistant, Nathan Green, moved to stand beside her. 'Yes he was joking,' he confirmed. 'Don't worry, you'll get used to the professor.'

The nurse simply gave a puzzled shake of her head and returned to her duties, leaving Dr Green staring at his mentor with obvious approval. The trouble with the young doctor, however, was that not only did he have admiration for his superior, he also had an outright desire for his wife.

~~~

How Tom ever found anything in the utter chaos of his office was a total mystery. Although he would try to convince people that there was some sort of system to
~~~

his paperwork, he had to concede it wasn't a particularly efficient one. In Major Richard Raven's office, on the other hand, the absolute opposite was true: it was neat, orderly and pristinely clean. Along the wall behind his desk was a row of photographs showing faces, all harrowing depictions of facial injuries suffered by soldiers, airman and sailors who were now his patients. Beneath each photo was an artist's drawing capturing the most exacting detail, and below that, a part-painted cellulose acetate sheet the major had created, which he used as an overlay to show how corrective surgery might look.

Tom paced up and down studying the various watercolours and pastels, waiting for Raven to return for their three o'clock meeting. It was the detail that fascinated Tom, and was the thing he couldn't help but study intensely, although the drawings were anything but pleasant viewing.

He placed an acetate sheet over a picture. Suddenly the face, although far from perfect, would at least be considered as acceptable by society. Tom heard the door open but was too engrossed to look around.

'I've got to hand it to you, Richard, how you can visualise making good out of this carnage constantly amazes me,' he said, pulling his eyes into a squint in order to look at a gaping void in a face where a nose had once been.

'Simply a process of playing with different surgical options, Tom. You know that,' replied Major Raven, walking into his office.

Tom finally turned towards his colleague. 'Yes, but my options are always limited. Here it's different. Things are infinitely possible.'

'Which is why I want you to work with me more. Help take reconstructive surgery to a whole new level.' He gave Tom an expectant look. 'Well, what about it? Have you given any more thought to joining me when we move to Sidcup?'

Giving an appreciative smile, Tom sat down. 'The offer's tempting, I won't deny it, but you know that I am committed to St Thomas's. And besides, I want to focus more on neuroscience when this war is over. Why our minds do as they do, that's my real passion.'

'I know,' Raven said in resigned tone, '… but I will keep trying to entice you.'

'In the meantime, you have me as much as time will allow,' Tom reassured him.

The pair were pouring over patient files discussing the proposed operation schedule for the next few days when a polite knock came on the door. The pair looked round to be greeted by a nurse accompanying a middle aged man wearing a shabby-looking suit and holding a leather document case.

'The gentleman you agreed you'd see this afternoon, Major Raven,' explained the nurse before making her exit.

'Of course, yes Mr …,' he stumbled. The look of awkwardness on the major's face showed that he'd totally forgotten his appointment, something highly unusual for Raven.

The man at the door saved him any further embarrassment. 'Dakin, sir. We spoke on the telephone.'

'Indeed, of course,' remembered Raven. 'Please take a seat …. Well, it all sounded a bit cloak and dagger, Mr Dakin, I have to say.'

Much as Tom was intrigued, he felt his presence was intrusive, so he got up out of his chair. 'Why don't I pop back and see you later, Richard.'

He was quite surprised to hear the response from the visitor: 'No, do stay, Professor Sharpe.'

'Forgive me, but do we know each other?' asked Tom.

'Not personally, but we do know all about you.'

'Sorry, I don't play cat and mouse,' Tom immediately batted back, annoyed at the man's attitude.

'Very well, gentlemen,' said Dakin and began to explain the purpose of his visit.

Dakin was part of Unit A, a branch of MO5(g) that had been set up within the secret service bureau to investigate espionage activity. For the last six months he had been working on Project Red Cross – an initiative based on the suspicion that German intelligence had infiltrated branches of the medical services and recruited various professionals as spies. Until now enemy agents had had only limited success in carrying out their espionage activities. However, more recently, significant progress had been made in obtaining intelligence of British military operations. The belief was that secrets had been coded and sent back and forth, without suspicion, using the surgical bags dispatched on a weekly basis to field doctors and surgeons in France. These bags, containing extensive material on new procedures, drugs and the latest information on medical experiments, also contained previously used artists' pictures, which Raven wanted to pass on to surgeons in the field in the hope they would be of some help in the immediate treatment of terrible facial injuries caused by shrapnel. The trouble was, nobody in the bureau could work out just how the code worked, or indeed what pieces of information had been passed on by using it. It was Dakin's job to find out.

'Let me get this straight. Are you accusing us of being spies?' said Raven indignantly.

Dakin gave a condescending false smile. 'I hardly think I would be talking to you here if that was the case, sir.'

It had only been a couple of minutes since his arrival, but already Tom had taken a dislike to the man.

Dakin continued, 'No, we know who the spy is.'

'Then who is it?' quizzed Raven.

'In good time, major.'

Tom let out a loud sigh of exasperation. 'Look, Mr Dakin, we are both extremely busy surgeons and shortly needed in theatre. If you could please come to your point.'

Unruffled, Dakin took off his wire-rimmed spectacles, breathed heavily on the lenses, and polished them, before opening his case and pulling out a batch of documents. He handed them over for viewing. 'For several weeks we provided staff with false information – even typists and the post room clerks who put the bags together. Then, we simply sat back to see what information got leaked.'

Tom offered a staged look of anticipation for the conclusion of Dakin's theatrical performance.

'... The leak, gentlemen, came from an artist in your studio called Wilson,' Dakin eventually confirmed. 'We fed him some false naval intelligence about a new weapon at Chatham. It was planted to look as if he'd stumbled on it by accident in some poster examples.'

Both Raven and Tom instantly looked out of the window and over towards the studio, where an innocent looking young man was busy at work painting a picture.

'Arthur Wilson! I can't believe it! He's my head artist. A nicer chap you couldn't wish to meet,' Raven exclaimed.

'Nice doesn't make him less dangerous or disillusioned with our country, major,' reminded Dakin.

Raven puffed out his cheeks. 'Now what happens?'

'We wait.' The reply was categorical. Relaxing slightly, Dakin carried on, 'Our people will continue to work on the code, and when we do eventually crack it, we'll use it to our advantage.'

One thing was puzzling both surgeons: why had they been told at this stage? Dakin was no amateur; he wouldn't risk his whole operation unnecessarily. Surely he could have waited for matters to reach a conclusion before telling them?

'Isn't it a risk, the two of us being aware of everything?' asked Tom.

Dakin gave a succinct clarification. 'I don't share any information unless I'm forced to, Professor Sharpe. But I need to interfere constantly with the content of those bags. I can only do that with your knowledge and help.'

From the ensuing silence, it didn't take much to realise the future relationship between the two men and Dakin would be a tense one.

Chapter 5

For the past two days Tom had laboured virtually around the clock, but war had no respect for working hours. Today had been particularly brutal, with sixteen emergencies being added to the eleven operations already planned. Looking at the names crossed through on the board outside the theatre brought home the reality of how badly the day was going. Pulling his mask down, he watched as the nurse pulled the sheet up over the soldier's face. 'Sorry ol' son,' he muttered and signed the sheet thrust in front of him. He couldn't help thinking how young the boy looked. In fact, he reckoned the eight patients that hadn't made it so far today wouldn't have had an average age of more than nineteen years.

It wasn't often that his job got Tom down, but at this moment he needed to take a break. A decent kick at the bottom of a door in the corridor opened it onto a fire escape. The sudden burst of sunlight made him squint and cover his eyes. The breeze danced across his face. 'Ah, fresh air!' He stood with eyes closed and breathed deeply.

Breaking into his few precious moments of tranquility

a voice said, 'The nurse said I might find you here.'

Still leaning his head back against the wall, he slowly opened his eyes and turned. 'Hello, Nathan.'

'Getting to you, today is it?' asked the professor's assistant and junior consultant.

'Aye, something like that,' Tom replied wearily, pushing himself off the wall and upright.

'I can do all the prep for the next one if you'd like.'

'No. Why don't you join me and take five minutes as well?'

Tom's invitation was eagerly accepted as it presented the young assistant with an opportunity on two levels. Firstly, it gave him the chance to pursue previous conversations about gaining experience by working in Major Raven's pioneering department. With every day that passed Green became more desperate to realise his ambition of becoming a facial reconstruction surgeon. Secondly, an opportunity to talk with Tom always meant the possibility of finding out more about his wife, Mary. Ever since seeing her photograph, when he first started to work under the professor, Green had been captivated by her beauty. It was not long before the idea of Mary Sharpe had become an obsession with him.

To most observers, and especially to Tom, Green was an enthusiastic young consultant, seemingly from a wealthy background, but unaccountably over eager to impress. His exuberance and flattery towards Tom, whilst annoying on occasions, were accepted because Nathan was a brilliant, talented and upcoming surgeon. Without a doubt, Tom's life at work was made a great deal easier by having the young doctor at his side.

Behind Green's enthusiastic exterior, however, lay a very complex and confused individual: complex in terms of ideology, politics, thoughts and beliefs; confused in his behaviour. Observing his slightly effeminate public schoolboy manner, one might easily assume Green to be homosexual; but he certainly wasn't. In fact, it often seemed that the contrary was true, for it was not unusual to find him flirting with the nursing staff and fuelling gossip about his female relationships.

Educated at Harrow, Green was part of a wealthy German family of industrialists. Green's father had settled in London towards the end of the nineteenth century, and had quickly established a company manufacturing medical equipment that seemed to be as successful as his relations' business in Germany. Before long, the father had bought a grand house in Belgravia, but then disaster struck: both parents were killed, and Green's younger sister was seriously maimed, in a house fire that took place whilst Green was away at medical college. Despite a thorough investigation, Green refused to accept the authorities' findings that the fire was accidental. He always suspected foul play by city financiers, to whom his father had still owed a considerable amount of the money he had borrowed to start his business and buy his home.

When the bank foreclosed on the father's debt, Green was forced to sell the damaged property at a fraction of its true value. He soon became consumed by a loathing for financial institutions, and it was only a promise that he'd made to his parents to succeed as a surgeon that stopped him from entering the underworld of financial crime to settle his score.

At college, the disillusioned student doctor was easily drawn towards a group of political activists. Within months, he was involved in some very questionable and violent behaviour. It was at this time that Green also started to develop his appetite for women, and quickly acquired a reputation as a Casanova. The only person he genuinely cared about was his sister Maude, who lived with him in their modest rented house in the north of the city. Much to Green's resentment, the house was all they could afford following the final settlement of their father's estate. To add further to his bitterness, the young doctor knew that more money would be needed to help alleviate Maude's problems in the longer term. Her face had been terribly disfigured by the fire that had ravaged the family home. The once beautiful sister now hid herself away inside her room, suffering pain and anguish.

Watching Tom draw his palms across his forehead

to release the tension, Green remarked, 'You really are working too hard. Tell you what, why don't I take you and Mrs Sharpe out one evening. We'll go up west and see a show?'

Not really seeing the offer as anything other than a lavish gesture that would probably never come off, Tom smiled and agreed, 'Why not?'

Green, on the other hand, was very serious about the offer. To him, it was a game his privileged education had prepared him for, and one he still very much wanted to play.

Just occasionally Tom liked to show his protégé he still had much to learn, particularly about the skill of handling people. Entering the corridor from the fire escape, the pair came across a young soldier lying on a stretcher waiting to be taken into the theatre. Obviously petrified, the young man was dragging continually on a cigarette he'd managed to acquire from a bearer.

'What do you think you're doing, soldier? You can't smoke here,' Green snapped.

Tom took control. Looking first at the soldier's notes and then at his injuries, he took hold of one end of the stretcher and gestured Green to take the other. Then they stretchered the man over to the fire escape and placed him on the floor again. Tom kicked open the door and winked at the soldier. 'There you go, quick as you can, eh? Then we can get you patched up.' A very grateful man really surprise Tom any more about the lengths people would go to in order to hide the truth.

Raven sat back in his chair and rolled a pencil through his fingers. 'I've been giving some thought to how he's managing it, you know – the coded messages.' He picked up a watercolour of a face Wilson had done and began studying it hard. Finally, he gave a defeated look. 'But it beats me.'

'Why don't we just wait and see what Dakin's people come up with. They'll find the truth eventually. It might turn out that it's nothing to do with Arthur in the end,' Tom declared, more out of hope than conviction. He liked Wilson, and often shared a joke or two with him when they met.

Seeing his colleague shake his head to indicate his thoughts had moved on, he decided to change the subject, although he suspected Raven was too preoccupied to pay full attention to anything he might say. 'Listen, Richard. One of the reasons I dropped by was to see whether you can use a bright new consultant I've got called Nathan Green. He's proving to be an absolute marvel with a scalpel, and keen to get involved in anything new and exciting. I'm sure you could use him and it would take a bit of pressure off me.'

Surprisingly the major was listening and appeared

quite positive about the proposition.

'Of course, yes. Have him pop by and see me … when it's convenient for you.'

Little could Tom have anticipated how flawed the decision to introduce Green to Raven would prove to be.

Chapter 6

Dakin's office was located on the third floor of Adelphi Court, which had been acquired for the ever increasing staff and activities of MO5(g). Outside, it looked exactly like what it was: a block of flats which had been converted into offices. Inside, it was a hive of activity with people squeezed into small rooms and surrounded by mountains of paperwork waiting to be indexed and filed. The registry, Unit C as it was known, was located just along the corridor from Dakin's office and was the bane of his life. The constant chatter from the exclusively female staff drove him mad. He slammed his door shut. Dakin was nothing if not sexist, bigoted, and miserable. He was also a man under pressure. So far this year, they had not caught even one spy.

Originally a detective within the police special branch, Dakin had been seconded to the new war office department at the start of the war in order to help investigate people suspected of being German spies. Three years on, the thrill of working here had gone. Now, he felt it was all form filling and card indexing.

'Heaven forbid I should get my intelligence blacklist sub-categorisation wrong, my dear,' was his favourite condescending retort to a query from Emily Dewhirst, one of the senior secretaries assigned to him.

The brave and brazen secretary, though, would often get the better of Dakin and his patronising ways. Once, on returning from being asked to retrieve an expenses folder he'd filed, she remarked, 'Sorry I've been so long, Mr Dakin, I wrongly assumed it was filed under Richard and not Dick!' Despite all his protests and a request to the lady superintendent to have the secretary dismissed, Emily remained in her position, mainly because she was simply brilliant at her job and one of the rising administrators of the department.

Today, Dakin was hoping for some good news. The results were back from the extensive chemical tests which had been done on the picture from the hospital. Emily handed over the package and left him to his business. She hadn't got very far down the corridor when she heard, 'Shit!' shouted loudly from Dakin's office. What he thought might happen turned out to be the case: the report was stamped 'TESTS INCONCLUSIVE – no evidence of invisible inks or materials likely to produce any element of known enemy code.'

Frustrated, Dakin flung the picture across his office and flopped into his chair. Eventually, he got back on his feet and made his way over to an area of the floor, where numerous items were placed carefully around a large leather bag. Squeezing his second finger and thumb across his forehead, he grimaced and muttered, 'Where is it?' Perhaps the code wasn't in the picture after all, he thought, and he started to look again at all the documentation surrounding the bag. But ultimately nothing was different to the hundreds of other times he'd checked before. 'You think you're clever, Wilson, but I will get you,' he vowed.

His bad morning was about to get much worse with a summons to room 56 on the floor above. A quick rap with his knuckles on the solid door brought the usual response, 'Yes.' Dakin slowly turned the handle and entered. The man he simply knew as 'C' seemed to take an eternity to look up and finally speak. 'The Admiralty chewed off my arse earlier today, Dakin. Why do you think that might be?' But Dakin wasn't allowed to even attempt an answer before his superior carried on, 'Because certain people in Whitehall think that my bloody department can't get their act together – stop secrets being leaked.'

Only after suffering several minutes of verbal assault and being told in plain language about his inadequacies did Dakin learn the news that two more ships had been sunk by U boat attacks. Both, apparently, as a consequence of German agents learning of their movements well in advance.

Stomping back to his office, Dakin felt hurt and furious in equal measure. One thing was certain: what rolled down would keep rolling down. 'Miss Dewhirst!' he bellowed.

~~~

News of the naval attacks fed front page headlines, and the newspapers clearly showed the mood of the nation. Propaganda was rife: 'Britain always has commanded the seas, and must continue to do so.' This was a sentiment that Dakin reminded Raven of during their short conversation on the telephone. The major reacted by silently mimicking him.

'Hello!' shouted a confused Dakin.

Eventually, the major decided to acknowledge him, 'Yes, I'm here.'

'Oh, right. I was saying, it's time I had a chat with your artist, Wilson. Can you arrange a meeting on the basis that I'm investigating a theft? Perhaps say some expensive stores materials have gone missing. I'll work the conversation round from there.'

'Yes, very well,' agreed Raven, although without much enthusiasm.

When Dakin visited the studio, even though his
~~~

questioning was subtle and cleverly done, Wilson's suspicions were immediately aroused. He sensed something was amiss and knew he would need to suspend his activities as quickly as possible. Becoming cautious about his every move, almost to the point of paranoia, the artist was convinced he was being watched. Indeed he was, for Dakin had had him and his home under intense surveillance for the last two months. But there was nothing about Arthur Wilson that would give the authorities any reason to arrest him: nothing suspicious about his correspondence, which was being intercepted and analysed; no covert meetings with anybody; no questionable telephone calls. Also, his background stood up to the most rigorous scrutiny, which was not surprising because all the facts were true, except for one – his origins.

Unbeknown to Dakin's investigators, Wilson had been born in South Africa and brought to England illegally by an uncle at the age of seven, following the death of his Burgher parents in the second Boer war. His father died in battle against British forces and his mother perished in one of the concentration camps set up to prevent farmers supplying food to the Boer commandos. A young Piet Kouch was renamed Arthur Wilson and quietly adopted by family friends. The trauma of that time never left him, but it was only at the age of sixteen, when told the true facts of his past, that he began to understand his nightmares. By the time he started his studies at Glasgow College of Art, his mistrust of British political policy was beginning to turn towards hatred. A chance meeting in 1912 with student Ingrid Schroeder, who had herself been recruited by German spymaster Gustav Steinhauer, offered a way for him to do something about his disillusionment.

Chapter 7

Two men at opposite ends of the country were about to feel the wrath of their wives, all thanks to Elliott's inventive plan.

'I simply can't believe it!' exclaimed Ann.

Elliott really couldn't see what all the fuss was about, but equally, he could see that his wife wasn't going to let things drop.

'Can't believe it,' she repeated, shaking her head.

'I thought —'

'But that's just it, Robert, you don't think, except when it suits you.'

'It's only two weeks, possibly three.'

'Only!'

Elliott leant his hand over the arm of the chair towards the gramophone.

'Don't even think about playing that thing!' Ann's swift reaction stopped him in his tracks. Shaking her head once more, she carried on, 'Whatever will I say to her?'

'It was only a suggestion, Ann. It wasn't written in stone … well not quite. All right, perhaps I should have talked it through with you first.'

The glare from his wife told him that was an understatement.

In London, a similar conversation was taking place between Tom and Mary.

'You've agreed to do what?'

'I didn't think you'd mind. Besides, we do need —'

'Tom, you never cease to amaze me … And how exactly do you envisage this arrangement is going to work?'

What Elliott had agreed with Tom, without any consultation with their wives, was that Mrs Sowerby and Daniel should go and stay with the Sharpes in London for a while. And, to add fuel to the fire, the pair had also agreed that Elliott and Ann would stay for a few days as well.

It was classic Elliott: here's the problem; here's the solution. For the male of the species, it couldn't have been simpler. For the female, it was one more lesson in always expecting the unexpected from your spouse.

Ann's phone call to Mary was very much like a book she was reading, the start being highly apologetic; the middle full of bewilderment and annoyance; and the end offering acceptance. After twenty minutes of talking, she finally replaced the ear piece of the telephone and went back into the parlour in search of her husband – whom she found had miraculously disappeared!

Leaving aside the lack of consultation, and the

ludicrous timetable, Elliott's plan was actually quite sensible. Tom and Mary had recently lost their cook-housekeeper, so Mrs Sowerby could conveniently fill that void. The inclusion of Daniel, however, would normally have scuppered the deal; but to Tom this merely added fascination and a chance for him to observe a medical condition of which he had not had much experience. As for Mary, her instinct was always to help those in need whenever she could. The whole situation tugged at her heart, and even though she had serious reservations about receiving strangers into her home, she would do her utmost to make them welcome.

Exactly how Daniel would react to such a move, even for a short period, would remain to be seen, although he had plenty of preparation from Mrs Sowerby. The inventive housekeeper devised a plan whereby, each evening, she would take the pack of cards off him after their little game and begin laying them out as the landmarks of London, whilst all the time emphasising that very soon they would be staying somewhere near these exciting places. On the third night she introduced a photograph of Tom, Mary and their baby Lucinda that Ann had provided. Then, in an attempt to link everything together, she started to explain about the train journey, describing a set of rules that he must follow. On retiring to bed that night, she discovered Daniel sitting on a mat with his toys and telling off all his soldiers, lined up as if they were passengers on the station platform.

'Daniel, what are you doing?' asked Mrs Sowerby softly but firmly.

Immediately becoming flustered, he replied 'The rule is that you give everyone a ticket, but they're boarding without getting one from you, Mrs Sowerby.'

Patiently she had to re-explain the rules.

~~~

Ernest Cooper's enquiries into who was the executor of Judge Sanderson's estate had been fruitful and the whole situation was now a lot clearer. The assumption that the judge had no relatives other than Daniel was correct, and the instructions he'd left to cover the eventuality of his death were that Peter Cribbs, a fellow judge from the West Riding circuit, should see that the terms of the will were carried out. Cooper, acting as the representative of Mrs Sowerby, made contact with Cribbs to clarify the situation regarding Daniel. Cribbs confirmed that he was aware of the mother's custody claim, but explained this was against the late Judge's wishes for Daniel. Sanderson's intention had been that the boy should remain under the care of Mrs Sowerby. As Cooper had expected would be the case, the outcome would need to be decided through
~~~

probate. In the meantime, Cribbs agreed to support Cooper's suggestion for Daniel to take the London break that had already been planned for him.

By the time the break came, Ann had fully embraced it, and whilst still having reservations about how it would all work out, she was thoroughly excited about going to London and seeing her friends, Tom and Mary – not to mention the opportunity to once more cuddle her goddaughter, Lucinda.

To Mrs Sowerby's great relief, her preparations with Daniel paid off, and all appeared to go well on the train journey. Her fear that he would become withdrawn and anxious proved wrong. In fact the opposite was the case, with Daniel suddenly and excitedly explaining to anyone who'd listen all about the landmarks of London, even though the elderly lady seated in the corner seemed to lose enthusiasm after being told about Nelson's Column for the twentieth time. Contrary to everything Mrs Sowerby thought would happen, the boy just accepted a total change in his routine. At the very least she'd expected a small tantrum.

It seemed that if anybody was going to throw a tantrum it was Elliott, whose dislike of being hemmed in made him irritable. Ann watched in amusement as the little elderly lady next to him kept moving her knitting wool and pattern further onto the small space between them. Eventually, he lost his patience. 'Would you like me to knit it for you, as well, dear?'

The woman just huffed at his rudeness and drew back her knitting, before eventually packing it away in favour of opening a tin and pulling out a sandwich. Elliott's face was a picture as the smell of onion began drifting up his nostrils.

Luckily, his daily paper was as yet unread, something Ann reminded him of with a smile whilst giving his foot a firm tap with hers to warn him not to create a scene. Elliott's response was to snap the newspaper in front of his face. The ensuing silence in the carriage was broken only by Daniel's regular outbursts of information until, at last, Mrs Sowerby began preparing him for their departure from the train. 'And what is the first rule when we arrive, Daniel?'

It was Mrs Sowerby, though, who forgot the rules. On stepping off the busy train onto an even busier platform, she became overwhelmed by the sheer pace of the movement around her and froze. The continuous noise ringing around her head made her feel unsteady. Back home in Sheffield she was used to loud noises, but here they were altogether different. In all her years, the furthest city she'd ever visited was Liverpool. She remembered that as being busy, but this place was almost too much to cope with. She clutched hard at Daniel's hand, making him flinch, whilst her other hand grabbed Ann's arm. The enormity of all that she was doing hit home. Her eyes grew wider and wider. Ann knew instantly that Mrs Sowerby was having a panic attack. She leant over and whispered very calmly in her ear, 'I'm here right behind you. Don't worry, everything is fine. I'll watch Daniel. You just take deep breaths.'

Moments later, Mrs Sowerby was back in control of herself. After taking an almighty deep breath, she exhaled slowly and looked at Ann with gratitude. 'Thank you,' she mouthed, without any sound. With that, she tugged at Daniel's hand and grinned. 'Told you it would be busy,' she said with confidence.

What had already been an eventful day saw one more incident before it was through. As the little group walked through the station to meet Tom and Mary, Daniel pulled them up by a theatre poster displayed on the wall to advertise a musical. The poster used a watercolour illustration full of vivid colour, and Mrs Sowerby thought the costumes probably reminded him of the uniforms of his soldiers. Conscious of needing to move on, she gently pulled at his hand, but Daniel stood firm, totally engrossed in the picture.

'Daniel, we need to be getting going. Come on,' she said, pulling his hand a little harder.

'No!' shouted Daniel, freeing his hand.

Mrs Sowerby didn't want a scene and at first tolerated this little outburst; but the boy quickly became quite agitated. Soon he was the centre of attention as people stopped to watch him clawing at the picture and shouting, 'No! Wrong! … Wrong!' It was a bizarre exhibition which didn't appear to make any sense.

Among the people watching, the expectation was that the boy would be shouted at, or even smacked, to make him stop. But Mrs Sowerby had learnt from experience this only made things worse. Despite the audible chorus of 'tuts', she continued to repeat his name calmly but firmly until he finally dropped his arms and turned to face her. Gently, she clasped his hands to reassure him. 'Everything's all right. Let's move on now.' His little round face took on an expression of acceptance and within minutes he'd archived the whole anxious episode in his memory.

Until now, neither Elliott nor Ann had fully appreciated the extent of Daniel's problems. Nor had Tom and Mary, who were standing, unnoticed, at a distance, watching the scene. However, neither seemed fazed by the prospect of what might lie ahead. If anything, their fascination and desire to help merely increased. What they did develop very quickly was an admiration for Mrs Sowerby.

Eventually the party arrived safely at the Sharpes' home near Finsbury Park, and it seemed that an arrangement potentially fraught with disaster actually worked very well from the start. Within hours of Mary showing Mrs Sowerby and Daniel to their rooms and giving them a tour of the house, the foundations of a good relationship were being laid. Once Daniel had settled into his room and was happily playing out the Battle of the Little Bighorn, Mrs Sowerby wasted no time in getting to grips with the Sharpes' kitchen, even to the point of preparing dinner for that evening. It was a far cry from the Sharpe's previous housekeeper, who had been almost unmanageable, and had decided to leave before she was dismissed.

Listening to Mrs Sowerby, Mary started to give a wry smile.

'What is it, Mrs Sharpe? Have I done something wrong?'

'Not at all,' Mary laughed. 'It's just hearing your accent. It's so reassuring.' She then spent the next five minutes recounting her days as a nurse in Sheffield and her affection for the place where she first met her husband.

'You make it all sound very romantic, Mrs Sharpe, but I'm afraid to me it's still a mucky old hole.'

Elsie Sowerby could be forgiven for feeling this way. Before beginning a hard life in service that had seen her rise to being Judge Sanderson's housekeeper, she remembered her neighbourhood of Sheffield only as squalid, poverty-stricken and full of desperate hardship. She didn't begrudge Mary her nice house and comfort; but she did wonder how her new mistress would cope in less pleasant surroundings. Never could she have imagined Mary as having spent time in Mesopotamia, and in the horrible conditions she'd endured there as a V.A.D nurse. Like most people, Mrs Sowerby was apt to judge a book by its cover.

Looking at her relatively young new housekeeper, Mary couldn't help wondering what might have happened to Mr Sowerby, although discretion stopped her asking the question, particularly in a time of war. If she had enquired, Mrs Sowerby would have explained that she had lost her husband at the beginning of the conflict. But actually this was far from the truth. Mrs Sowerby wasn't a married woman at all. The title was one that she had adopted for two reasons: to cover her feelings of anxiety at still being a spinster; and to make herself seem more suitable for a job as housekeeper. Pretending she had married her lover, who had subsequently been killed in battle, gave her a sense of normality and comfort.

At just over thirty three years of age, Elsie Sowerby had never really known love, and certainly not intimacy, or indeed any physical encounter. And yet she couldn't be considered unattractive. She had a pretty face and a trim figure that wouldn't have looked out of place in a group of much younger women. Also, given the chance, she always proved to be charming company. The one thing that Mrs Sowerby did have experience of, however, was infatuation. Peter Tyler had been a man whom she had very much wanted, but had told herself she couldn't have. By the time she realised this didn't have to be so, he had gone.

After that, her failure to find a sweetheart owed something to the isolation of the judge's rural property, to which there was little transport. Her childhood also played a large part, because her memories of her parent's relationship filled her with dread: her mother's life had been full of violence, abuse and humiliation. Finally, Daniel's total dependence on her had made forming other relationships difficult, although she accepted it willingly, and it fulfilled some of her emotional needs.

Distracted by a shout of 'Phew!' from the parlour, Mary went to investigate, only to find that Ann had taken baby Lucinda on her knee and was enjoying being able to have precious time with her goddaughter without any disruption from her own two boys, Henry and Cecil. She had just been wondering when she might be able to get her mother down again from Scarborough to look after the pair when a little faux pas by the restless bundle in her arms brought her back to reality. 'Phew! And I see nothing has changed with you, little one!'

Chapter 8

Being in the company of different people was enough to bring about a sudden and welcome change in Daniel. After only three days' stay in his new environment, he was beginning to explore his surroundings, as well as his newfound skills in interacting with people. In particular, he had accepted and taken to Mary very well, probably because she was female and whenever she spoke to him her voice replicated Mrs Sowerby's reassuring tone.

Daniel was also very curious about the gorgeous little girl who, most of the time, appeared to be attached to Mary's waist. Undoubtedly, Lucinda was growing up to be as beautiful as her mother, with unblemished matte olive skin and thick dark hair which was already beginning to hang with a wave like Mary's. Always with her thumb in her mouth, the infant let her little dark nut-brown eyes follow Daniel around whenever they all gathered in a room. Her occasional mischievous smile made him even more fascinated.

Of course Daniel was fully aware of babies and toddlers, but seldom in the last five years, had he had contact with any. This indicated the extent of his isolation and the protective bubble that had been created by his father and Mrs Sowerby.

One afternoon, standing unnoticed by a slightly ajar bedroom door, Daniel watched in amazement as Mary fed baby Lucinda from a bottle. His eyebrows knitted together in confusion, as he wondered why the child was wrestling with a long container of white fluid. Unfurling his brow, he opened his eyes wide, trying to comprehend why she was now being placed over Mary's shoulder and having her back rubbed. The resulting little burp made him giggle.

'Why don't you come in, Daniel?' asked Mary, realising that she was being secretly watched.

Eventually he peered around the door to see Mary smiling broadly at him.

'Hello, young man.'

He didn't answer. Instead he was more interested in Lucinda, who had drifted into a slumber and was motionless. Again he drew his eyebrows as one. Watching Mary continue to stroke the baby's back, he innocently asked, 'Now that you've killed her, will that bring her back to life?'

It took a moment for Mary to grasp Daniel's perception of what was going on. 'Oh! I see. You thought —,' but she stopped herself, realising how the situation must look to a child who could only interpret situations quite literally. 'Here. Have a seat on the couch,' she said kindly, patting the space next to her. 'I will explain things to you.'

Daniel didn't object and sat down. For the first time he appeared willing to listen and take instruction from a woman other that Mrs Sowerby.

Mary pulled Lucinda away from her shoulder and laid her backwards on her knees. To Daniel's astonishment the baby stretched and opened her eyes. 'It worked!' he shouted excitedly, 'She's not dead!'

'No, not at all. You see, Lucinda was only asleep …'

Daniel found Mary's explanation of how to wind a baby totally fascinating, and his expression of curiosity made Mary realise just how much she missed her work with deaf children. Her thoughts drifted momentarily back to Sheffield, as she remembered the many happy hours she had spent teaching sign language at the deaf school there.

'Perhaps you would like to help?' enquired Mary, allowing her precious memories to fade. 'You could carry on feeding Lucinda for me.'

'Can I?' blurted out Daniel excitedly, his eyes opening as wide as they could. He wriggled his backside on the couch to get comfy and comically held out his arms in anticipation.

'Now it's really important to be gentle.'

Daniel nodded his head continually in agreement and eagerly waited to take the bundle. Eventually he did, albeit somewhat awkwardly.

Mary handed him the bottle. 'Softly press this bit to her lips,' she instructed 'and she'll take it in and start feeding.' But true to her character, Lucinda had no intention of playing along and kept flicking the teat out of her mouth.

What Mary had yet to fully realise was Daniel's patience threshold, which was far lower than that of most other children his age. Without warning he stood up, stating, 'I've had enough of her now,' and tossed Lucinda casually onto the couch behind him, as if she were one of his toys.

'Daniel!' shrieked Mary, in alarm.

Mary's shouting startled him. That and Lucinda's sudden loud crying sent him into a blind panic. He stood there shaking. It was all too much for him to understand what was wrong. Soon came the continuous rocking and tapping of his head. 'Don't like the noise … take the noise away!' he repeatedly cried.

The whole commotion quickly brought Mrs Sowerby onto the scene. Instinctively, she took control, and wrapping her arms tightly around Daniel, she rocked him whilst whispering, 'It's all right … everything is all right.' Firmly, she clasped her hand around his to stop him now trying to tap his leg.

As quickly as things had flared up, they died down. Within a matter of minutes nobody would have ever known there had been a crisis – Lucinda was chuckling away in Mary's arms and Daniel was asking when they were due to eat.

Mrs Sowerby puffed out her cheeks, 'I am so sorry, ma'am. I don't know what happened, but I am so sorry.'

'Please, Mrs Sowerby,' said Mary, holding up a hand to silence her, 'I'm afraid this is entirely my fault, not Daniel's. You see, we were just …'

~~~

About to enter the study, both Tom and Elliott paused at the door in surprise. Inside stood Daniel, studying different paintings of faces spread out on the desk. He appeared so engrossed, and with one picture in particular, that he didn't even hear or sense the presence of anyone nearby. Again and again he kept coming back to the same watercolour, holding it up and gazing hard at it, although it wasn't as if the content was any different to that of any other picture. They all depicted the same, disturbing, facial disfiguration of soldiers.

Daniel's reaction was to scratch anxiously at the picture, in the same way he had at the poster at the railway station, only this time he did something different,
~~~

and seemingly without reason. Calmly, he held the picture aloft and pretended to draw a series of lines over it with his finger. The lines were short and went in all directions, some definite and fast, others slow and uncertain. Occasionally he would stop, appearing to change his mind. Then, after some serious thought, he would begin furiously scrubbing out his imaginary lines before starting the process all over again.

Whilst Tom was transfixed, trying to understand the boy's behaviour, Elliott, who didn't really have much appreciation of how differently Daniel needed to be dealt with, decided to speak out, and with his usual straight-to-the-point approach. 'Now you just be careful with those, lad,' he said sternly, as if talking to one of his sons.

Tom huffed in despair. Despite the pair being good friends, Tom was invariably left frustrated by Elliott's uncompromising style. He held up his hand to indicate that he wanted to handle the situation.

'That man was a good, brave soldier, Daniel. Not unlike one of Custer's cavalrymen against Sitting Bull's Indians.'

Daniel immediately turned round. Not because he was disturbed, but purely because of the words he'd heard. Once more, his eyebrows drew towards each other. Never before had anyone, other than Mrs Sowerby, spoken to him about General Custer or the Sioux.

Having previously studied Daniel at play, Tom had

realised that to gain the boy's attention when he was in a heightened state of anxiety, he needed to be diverted back to his toys and familiar patterns of play. 'I've an atlas over here. Perhaps we could show Mr Elliott where the battle took place?' Tom suggested. It worked; Daniel became like putty in Tom's hands and enthusiastically followed him over to the bookcase.

'There you go, Mr Elliott,' announced Tom, pointing to a page before continuing the game in a school-teacher fashion. 'The battle took place in a state of America called Montana. Isn't that right, Daniel?'

Even though he found the situation a little patronising, Elliott played along and nodded like an attentive student, allowing Daniel to pass on his considerable and impressive knowledge of the subject. The conversation, though, ended abruptly when Daniel asked indignantly, 'Did you not know all that?' After which, he disappeared out of the study.

Elliott looked somewhat shocked. Very rarely did a child have the last word with him. 'Well, excuse me!' he remonstrated, whilst pulling a face.

Tom sniggered. 'Come on, Mr Elliott, keep up will you,' he mocked. 'Did they not teach you history at that school of yours?'

Even Elliott had to laugh. 'Obviously not!'

With Daniel now gone, Tom looked for a medical

report on delinquency, which he knew would be of interest to Elliott, who was wandering round the study picking up and attempting to make sense of medical notes. 'Es … o … ph … a … something or other,' he muttered. 'Esophageal motility dysfunction,' Tom confirmed with a smile, knowing that his friend would be none the wiser. 'It's a serious condition with the throat.'

'Is it? Why can't you just put that then, instead of making it sound like a Greek tragedy?'

Was there any point in even attempting a response, Tom wondered.

'What do you make of the lad's behaviour with these paintings, then?' asked Elliott, approaching the desk. But before Tom could give an answer, Elliott had picked up one of the pictures. 'Oh, good grief,' he moaned, seeing the disturbing content. 'No wonder the boy was unsettled. What are they?'

Tom didn't immediately answer. He was preoccupied with retrieving the report from amongst the piles of paperwork chaotically spread on the bookcase. In fact, there was paperwork strewn everywhere. Mary had long ago given up any hope of her husband keeping his study tidy and therefore chose never to go in, preferring to pretend that the room simply didn't exist. Finally, he turned over some papers and found the report. 'Ah, here it is …. Sorry, Robert, what were you saying?'

'These paintings, they're distressing.'

It had never really occurred to Tom that people might find the depictions of horrific injuries distressing. To him, blood, gore and disfigurement were all part of his daily routine.

'Yes, I suppose to some people they are. I should really keep them out of view. It's just that, well, normally nobody ever comes in here apart from me.'

'Sounds utter bliss!' sighed Elliott.

'Listen, Robert,' Tom's tone suddenly became quite serious. 'I need to have a word with you about these pictures … and very much in confidence.

Chapter 9

From behind his draughtsman's board, Wilson nervously tapped a pencil against his raised thumb. He couldn't concentrate properly; his mind was just too full of questions. When would it be safe enough for him to continue? Should he continue at all? Why not just pack up and go, disappear into the city and find another life? But deep down, he knew that wasn't a viable option – they'd find him and then what? All he could think off was the fate of poor Beatson. The image of his awful demise sent a shudder down the artist's spine. He stopped tapping and looked down at his bright red thumb, now beginning to really hurt.

'For heaven's sake, calm down,' he said to himself and took a deep breath. He knew he would be safe as long as they needed his painting skills. After that, well, the situation would be different. Then, he'd almost certainly be killed. Again, he began tapping with his pencil. The problem for Wilson was that he knew too much!

Out of the corner of his eye, he sensed that he was being watched. Indeed he was. From the office opposite,

Major Raven, with Nathan Green by his side, peered into the studio.

'Arthur Wilson, he's my head artist,' said Raven, handing the young consultant surgeon a couple of pictures. 'Responsible for these.'

The man took the drawings, showing the likely results of surgery on a disfigured face, and marvelled at the detail, and the likeness to the procedures he had just witnessed, 'Quite extraordinary,' he commented. 'I must compliment him on his talent. As I must you, Major Raven,' he added, before turning towards Tom, who was sitting by the desk.

'... and of course you too, Professor Sharpe,' Green continued in his sycophantic manner. 'What I saw in theatre earlier today, gentlemen, was truly remarkable.'

Tom got out of his chair to join the pair by the window. Unlike Raven, he was used to his assistant's kow-towing and never wished to bask in his praises. 'Yes, well, all part of our calling to be surgeons, eh, Mr Green.'

'Indeed,' smiled Green, before turning his attention back towards Raven. 'So, Major, will it be possible to hone my skills under your excellent supervision?'

Tom rolled his eyes upwards in embarrassment. Raven, on the other hand, was clearly happy to keep receiving accolades.

'I'm sure if Professor Sharpe can spare you, then I

could utilise your obvious talents, Mr Green.'

Frowning at the pair's mutual appreciation of each other, Tom suggested, 'Shall we go and see the studio then?'

In the studio, watching the small party of men approach him, Wilson felt physically sick with apprehension. The more he tried to act normally, the more his behaviour appeared strange. Against his will, he began to twitch, as perspiration from his armpits began to trickle uncomfortably down the sides of his torso. He pushed his arms inwards to stop it, only for this to make him seem even more ill at ease.

'Everything all right, Mr Wilson?' asked the major, watching the artist uncharacteristically scratch himself.

'Yes, fine, sir!' insisted Wilson, attempting to stand still. 'Just seem to be suffering awful irritation these days. I don't know what it is.'

'Perhaps it's nothing more than a change of soap?' Green suggested in a slightly scornful tone.

Wilson gave a resentful look.

'This is Mr Nathan Green, a consultant with Professor Sharpe,' said the major. 'He'll be spending some time with me in theatre, so you will see him around here from time to time.'

'I see. Well, should there be anything I can do to assist you, Mr Green, don't hesitate to ask,' Wilson offered, although his words didn't exactly come across as warm and welcoming – something Tom immediately noticed.

Green wasn't put out by Wilson's slight hostility. Instead, he complimented the artist on his skilful work. 'I've seldom seen watercolours quite as exquisite.'

Given the content of the pictures, it was hard to see how anyone could class the pictures as exquisite. But Green seemed to be disturbingly attracted to them.

The major lifted his arm, gesturing the way forward to tour the rest of the dept. Although Tom held back, wanting to catch a quick word with the artist.

'I was wondering if I might take home a couple of your old drawings, Arthur. You know, ones from patients that unfortunately didn't make it.'

Wilson tried desperately not to look alarmed but couldn't help blurting out indignantly, 'Why?'

Tom knew there was something amiss with Wilson's behaviour, but he resisted using his position of superiority to get his way. Instead, he willingly explained. 'They simply allow me to study and compare the different outcomes of surgery properly.'

'I can't just —' began Wilson fiercely, before realising that his behaviour was only fuelling any suspicions of him the others might have. 'I'm sorry, Professor … Ignore me. I'm just tired. Like everyone else, I seem to do nothing but eat, sleep and drink this damn place.' He rubbed his furrowed brow, highlighting his anxiety. 'As you know,

Major Raven likes to send any unneeded pictures to the surgeons in the field. But I'm sure I can arrange to pull some back. Can you leave it with me for a while?'

'Sure,' Tom replied and patted Wilson's shoulder. 'It gets to us all at times, Arthur. Keep smiling, eh.'

Walking away, questions as to what Wilson could possibly be up to began bouncing around furiously in Tom's head, like a metal ball in a fairground bagatelle. As always, he knew the answer would eventually be found through simple logic. That and perhaps a little input from Elliott!

Just when the visit to the studio was coming to an end, the theatre recovery sister came up and interrupted the major, discreetly whispering in his ear.

'I see,' said the major with a look of despair. 'You'll have to excuse me, Mr Green, but I'm required on the ward.'

'Problem?' interrupted Tom. He guessed from the dejected look on the major's face that the conversation with the sister related to bad news following the operation on the wounded soldier earlier in the day.

'Exactly the same as last time,' sighed Raven.

Tom knew only too well how his colleague was feeling. However much a surgeon accepted the risks associated with pioneering new techniques, when things went wrong and a patient died, then the loss was felt quite personally. Offering Raven his help in analysing the facts,

Tom suggested they walk together towards the ward.

Left alone, Green and Wilson cautiously looked each other up and down. 'All par for the course when you're a pioneer like the major, eh?' suggested Green to the artist, as they watched Raven and Tom disappear round the corner.

'You bastard!' Wilson forced his unexpected response through clenched teeth. 'Where the hell have you been for the last two weeks?'

'Calm down now, Arthur. We don't want to arouse any more suspicion than there already is,' replied Green coolly, an unsettling false smile on his face. He took hold of Wilson's arm and firmly guided him to his chair.

The two men began to talk in hushed tone, with Green occasionally looking over to Wilson's colleagues and giving them a supposedly reassuring smile.

'They know everything. We need to meet to —' the artist tried to say, but was cut short.

'No! There's no need to panic.'

Wilson fumbled with his cigarette packet, eventually pulling one out and shakily putting the tip in his mouth. 'Don't panic! For God's sake, Nathan, we're on the verge of being discovered,' he stuttered, trying to speak and light the cigarette at the same time. 'We need a way out, and quickly.'

Green didn't care for being spoken to in such a manner. 'Pathetic!' He derided his colleague, whilst directing a sinister glare deep into the man's worried eyes. 'You really are pathetic, Wilson.' It was only out of his own dedication to spymaster, Steinhauer's programme that he continued to tolerate Wilson's failings.

'No, I'm just a realist,' answered back Wilson, finding the courage to stand up to the man whom, despite his slight frame, he always found intimidating.

'Realist?' scoffed Green. 'Coward more like.' He reached out and squeezed the artist's fingers together tightly. Only when Wilson grimaced enough for the other artists to look over towards them, did he release his pressure. 'But it will be our little secret, eh, Arthur. There's no need for people to know the real truth about you.'

Wilson forcibly pulled his hand away and nursed his aching fingers. Eventually, he responded to his aggressor. 'Nor is there any reason for people to know the truth about you, my dear Nathan!'

As soon as he'd said the words, he wished he hadn't, because Green was the nastiest and most vindictive man that he had ever met, and, he was now sidling up closer to him, with a look of sheer contempt. 'Remember the room!' he said with morose meaning. Instantly, Wilson's thoughts returned to that dark and tragic room etched in his mind; the place with a lone chair reeking with the horrible smell of urine and blood, a room with an atmosphere full of panic and fear, where he had watched, in shock, at Green's torturing and brutal killing of a suspected informant.

Slowly, Wilson swallowed to relieve the dryness in his mouth. He certainly had no desire to ever again go anywhere near that chilling room, with its awful chair!

Chapter 10

Tom was in the doghouse again! And, on this occasion, he'd even trumped Elliott for not considering the impact of his actions. It was now six o'clock, and he had just strolled through the door and announced that he'd invited Nathan Green, along with Major Raven and his wife, for dinner at eight.

In fairness, it could be argued that Tom had been considering Mary when Green had mentioned he could get tickets for that evening's show at the Opera. He knew his wife cared nothing for that style of music. In fact, he himself wasn't much impressed with it either. To avoid giving offence, Tom had made an excuse about Mary having already seen the performance, and suggested that both Green and Raven should come for dinner instead. He never really expected they would accept his invitation at such short notice, but once they had, he had meant to telephone Mary to explain the situation, although, as was usual with Tom, his thought processes raced ahead like a steam engine onto something else, and he clean forgot. If a 'to do' task wasn't medical, then it invariably slipped down his list of priorities.

'For heaven's sake, Tom!' Mary's words were followed by an audible sigh. 'This really is you at your absolute finest, darling,' she added with sarcasm. 'How on earth do you expect —'

Mrs Sowerby interrupted, trying to be optimistic in the circumstances. 'I suppose I could always try to —'

'No. This just isn't fair. And what's more, my husband knows it. He's going to apologise to you, Mrs Sowerby,' declared Mary, folding her arms and looking towards her spouse with expectation.

Seeing Elliott and Ann pass in the hallway, Tom seized the opportunity to deflect any further hostility and make his exit. 'Ah, Robert!' he called. Then, with all the charm he could muster, he planted a kiss on his wife's cheek. 'Sorry, dear! I was going to telephone you at lunchtime but got sidetracked … You know how it is … And please do forgive me, Mrs Sowerby, I'm sure you'll come up with something.' He was out of the room before Mary even had time to think of a reply.

Mrs Sowerby could only stand desperately trying to think of how she could creatively spin out the available food for another three people, while Mary suddenly realised something else and flew into a panic, crying, 'Chairs!' With the additional guests, they would be two chairs short at the dinner table.

'Everything all right?' asked Ann, popping her head into the room as Tom dragged Elliott down the hall.

'I'm going to kill him … definitely going to kill him!' Mary muttered and gave the broadest of false smiles. 'You might just see a husband murdered tonight, Ann.'

'Ooh, I hope it's mine!' Ann joked, having herself spent most of the day bickering with Elliott over trivialities.

Soon all three women were laughing, whilst trying to pull together a plan of action. Luckily, at that point Major Raven telephoned to cancel, so, with only Nathan Green now expected, the pressure lifted considerably.

Mrs Sowerby used the light hearted mood to remind Mary that she was taking Daniel to the city the following day and wouldn't be available to help with Lucinda.

'Oh, yes I had forgotten. Thank you for letting me know.' Mary thought for a moment. 'Actually, there's something you could do for me whilst you're there. My rings are at a jeweller's on Bond Street for cleaning and re-sizing. Would you please pick them up? The shop isn't far from the underground station.'

'Of course, Mrs Sharpe.'

Had the atmosphere been rather less frosty when they were dressing for dinner, Tom might have mentioned to his wife about Nathan Green's ingratiating manner towards him, and warned her that he might act similarly with her. However, when Green arrived, he adopted a completely opposite approach. He deliberately made himself appear rather shy, with an almost mysterious quality; and when paying a compliment, he did so in a charming manner that could not in any way be considered fawning. He knew quite well how to reproduce the behaviour of a well-educated young Englishman.

On entering the sitting room and seeing Daniel at a table, Green stopped in his tracks, his expression quickly turning to one of fear. Studying the boy's face thoroughly, he became convinced: it was him!

Nervously playing with the cigarette case in his pocket, Green desperately wondered how to handle things. The problem was simple – if the boy was here, then so, most likely, was his nurse, Mrs So… something. Her actual name, he couldn't quite remember. What if they recognised him? It would all be over. Although the young consultant was reasonably confident of his disguise, he remained terrified of being discovered. Of course he could be wrong about the boy: he might only look similar.

'And this is Master Daniel, Mr Green,' explained Mary. 'He's staying with us temporarily.' She leant forward, raising her hand discreetly to muffle her voice, 'Unfortunately, he's recently lost his father.'

Her words merely confirmed to Green that he was right. But why would the boy be at Tom's house, he wondered.

'Oh dear,' he muttered, every bit the sympathetic visitor. 'And his mother?'

Mary shook her head and whispered, 'He only has a nurse.'

Now he was convinced beyond a doubt.

'And here are our very good friends, Robert and Ann Elliott,' continued Mary, turning to the pair. 'Mr Green works at the hospital with Tom.'

Ann gave a pleasant smile and nod of acknowledgment. Elliott rose from his seat and extended his hand. 'Mr Green,' he said, speaking in his formal and businesslike manner, and beginning to assess the considerably shorter man in front of him. About thirty years, he thought … Fresh faced but maturely groomed, except for that moustache – looks ridiculous! … Presentable in style … Assume he's highly intelligent, given his profession … Looks well-bred … Typical doctor …

Green, whose interest was elsewhere in the room, offered a not very enthusiastic handshake.

If a man can't do a handshake properly, then why do one at all, thought Elliott, and pushed home his point by squeezing harder and nearly crushing Green's fingers.

'Pleased to meet you, sir,' said Green, with a slight wince. Soon he had turned away from Elliott and was conversing in his more usual, brash, attention-grabbing manner.

Elliott had by now firmly formed his opinion – Cad!

Daniel seemed to be interested only in the two tin soldiers he was playing with when Mary asked, 'Daniel, are you going to say hello to Mr Green?'

Only after numerous repetitions of the question did the boy look up and say, 'Hello,' without any hint of emotion.

'Er …Yes, hello to you too,' replied Green, looking very uneasy. He was aware of the boy's problems, and therefore knew he could be unpredictable. What if he suddenly blurted something out?

'Is everything all right, Mr Green? You look very troubled all of a sudden,' commented Mary.

'Do I?'

When required to do so, Green could easily conjure up a lie, with an accompanying scenario, and act it out convincingly. 'I'm sorry,' he started, 'It's just that he looks so similar to a boy I was treating at the hospital.' Bowing his head slightly, he cast his eyes downwards. On lifting them again, they were tear-filled. 'Sadly, we lost him on Tuesday.'

'Oh, I am sorry.' Mary reached out her hand instinctively and touched his arm in a gesture of comfort. Her casual, yet genuine, touch sent a tingle of warm excitement through his body. Despite his many conquests, he couldn't remember the last time a woman had come close to making him feel the way he did at this moment.

All he wanted was her touch again. Suddenly, he was lost in a vivid fantasy, looking at Mary's half-naked body in a mirror, her beautiful long wavy hair discreetly covering her breasts. She shivered against the cool breeze in the room. His slender hands warmed and caressed her, then gently lifted away the locks of hair to expose her body to the intensity of his stare.

To Ann, at least, it seemed that for a few moments Green's interest was wholly fixed on Mary, and seeing how his eyes were devouring her friend, she preferred not to think what might be going through his mind. Soon, however, the guest was back with his more gregarious persona, and he began treating everyone to his humorous 'tales from the operating theatre'.

Elliott wasn't much impressed, but gave the odd smile to acknowledge the man's supposedly entertaining performance. He soon switched off completely from the stories, preferring instead to just observe. He became curious as to why Green kept glancing back over towards Daniel. And why, each time, did he look more nervous? Continuing to analyse the young surgeon, Elliott thought back to what the man had said to Mary. It all began to puzzle him, but it wasn't long before he'd established a theory.

Green could hardly fail to notice he was being studied. It was time to deflect attention onto somebody else, and the presence of Tom presented him with an ideal opportunity. 'Oh, Tom, I really must grab a quick word with you before dinner,' he called. Before moving on, however, he took hold of Ann and Mary's hands in turn and gave each a gentle kiss, gushing, 'A pleasure to meet you, ladies. Please excuse me.'

As false and unpleasantly ingratiating as Ann found Green, she was never beyond a bit of harmless flirting, particularly if there had been some flattery; and after the day she'd had with Elliott, she had every intention of using the opportunity to tease him. 'And that, my dear, grouchy husband, is how you need to treat a lady!' she declared.

Elliott indulged in some gruff and barely intelligible muttering.

'At least, if you want your socks darning for Monday,' she joked, straightening his tie and smiling. 'Come on, Mr Grumpy.'

Once Mary had seated her guests in the dining room, the opening of the door made everyone turn around and look. Mrs Sowerby entered, and immediately looked uncomfortable at feeling all eyes were upon her. The room fell silent – although not for any reason other than that the door suddenly opening had taken people by surprise.

'Aagh! But which one of us is really the murderer, Mrs Sowerby?' Tom joked. The laughter released her from an awkward situation.

She gave her own little nervous laugh before asking Mary, 'Are you ready for me to bring in the dishes, ma'am?'

'Of course. Please go ahead.'

Meanwhile, Green had braced himself. Although more than a year had passed, he feared there was every likelihood she would remember him. All he could do was take a deep breath and hope. When their eyes did finally meet, Mrs Sowerby merely gave the young surgeon a pleasant smile. If she had recognised him, she hid the fact very well. However, he could not take any chances. Mrs Sowerby had to be eradicated!

Chapter 11

Having endured Green's conversation at the dinner table, and afterwards in Tom's study, Elliott was thoroughly relieved when, finally, the front door closed on a man he was quite convinced was lying. When it came to spotting criminal intent, or just someone who had something to hide, Elliott seemed to have a sixth sense. This was the reason he was often asked to help the police with their cases. In truth, this intuition was probably nothing more than an astuteness gained from over 20 years observing and working with felons. Either way, he had serious doubts about Tom's smart young colleague, Nathan Green.

What had prompted Elliott's mistrust was Green's behaviour when telling the story of the boy in the hospital. It didn't make sense and he wanted Tom's opinion. His friend, however, seemed more interested in playing a juvenile game than talking. Stretching his legs over the corner of his desk, Tom had rested one foot on a pile of papers, haphazardly stacked about eight inches high. Then, wriggling his foot carefully, he tried to see if he could release it from his untied shoe without the papers falling over. Elliott watched dumbfounded. Here was an eminent professor of surgery playing silly beggars, and sticking his tongue out to one side of his mouth in fierce concentration, oblivious to everything around him.

Only after several minutes did Tom look up and realise his friend was gazing at him, unimpressed.

'How old are you?' asked Elliott, shaking his head.

'It's just a game we used to play at university, that's all,' said Tom defensively, and carried on like a mischievous child. Moments later his shoe fell to the ground. 'Dah, Dah!' he called out, swiftly pulling his leg off the table and grabbing the papers before they flew everywhere.

Elliott just frowned with indifference.

Like Ann, Tom had learnt to read between the lines with Elliott and to interpret his pattern of thought whenever he suddenly changed the subject. Therefore, he wasn't too surprised to hear his friend ask him totally out of the blue, 'Desensitization. What's your view?'

He gave the question some thought. 'Medically or generally?' he asked.

'Medically of course,' answered Elliott, looking somewhat shocked that he could have been misunderstood. 'Actually, let's be specific …'

Tom could only nod appreciatively.

'… Would you say, as a surgeon, you're desensitized?'

At last, Tom could begin to make sense of Elliott. The

question sent a series of scenes flashing through his mind; scenes from his time in Flanders dealing with the carnage of the battlefield; a gallery of brutal images which began racing faster and faster, until eventually he closed his eyes tightly and everything stopped. On opening them again, he stared into space, realising just how normal the suffering of war had actually become. 'Yes,' he confirmed. 'I'm desensitized, Robert. I have to be. Why do you ask?'

Elliott went on to explain his observations of Green's behaviour and particularly his reactions to Daniel's presence. He then went on to divulge his theory.

'He'd experience the same sort of heart breaking scenes as you and other surgeons, would he not?'

Tom gave a nod.

'... So would it not seem strange to you that he was tearful at losing a patient, even if it were a child?'

'Oh come now, Robert. You of all people know that you can't generalise like that. We all react differently to situations.'

But Elliott wasn't having any of Tom's rational thinking. He barely allowed his friend to finish before batting back his response. 'It's like when I visit detainees in the cells. Some often have harrowing tales to tell, and as much as I care about their plight, I never get emotional any more. Why? Because I'm so hardened to it all. You've just said it yourself – you become desensitized. It's the only way you get through. No, in my opinion, there is no boy. He was lying to Mary.'

Even though Elliott's opinion wasn't an altogether unreasonable one, Tom didn't look particularly convinced. Soon the pair were locked in a debate.

'But why would Green want to invent a situation like that?' asked Tom, the deep furrows beginning to appear on his forehead.

Elliott jumped in with his theory. 'Because something about seeing Daniel in your sitting room upset him. The question is what?'

In their professional relationship, invariably it was Tom who would first query the logic of a situation. On this occasion, however, he would admit that his friend had spotted something illogical that he hadn't paid much attention to. Even so, his instinct was still telling him that Green was probably doing no more than trying to make an impression on his wife with his story of the dead boy. What did bother him though, the more he thought about it, was that his colleague wasn't treating any children at the hospital, or at least none to his knowledge.

After talking about the matter for a while longer, the discussion ended with Tom agreeing to make enquires about the boy supposed to have died at the hospital. And, if necessary, he would casually quiz Green further. The rest of the evening was spent in conversation about even more intriguing things – such as Dakin's visit, the allegations of spying and secrets being leaked through a hospital department, and the possible involvement of one of the hospital artists. The information Tom shared he certainly shouldn't have, but he knew nobody was more trustworthy than Elliott. It all captured Elliott's wildest imagination. Ever since reading Le Queux's popular fantasies about 'spymania' in England some years before, he had hoped desperately that he might come across some espionage activity in his probation work. And now, here was Tom at the hospital involved first hand in events that the espionage writer himself would have been proud to write about. It made Tom smile to see Elliott all of a sudden acting like an excited little schoolboy.

Talk of the hospital artists brought them back to Daniel, and his reactions to the drawings. Tom had a theory he wanted to run by his friend regarding what, if anything, Daniel was seeing in the pictures and why he became agitated when viewing them. Looking at the foolscap piece of paper that Tom had given him, Elliott considered the surgeon's theory. It was an entertaining one, he wouldn't deny that. Whilst the sheet appeared to be nothing more than doodles or an abstract pattern at best, it really represented a series of lines which Tom had captured after watching Daniel in front of the pictures. Underneath was his interpretation of how the lines might represent a code. It all formed a bit of a crude hypothesis, but it was fascinating to Elliott.

'Have you shared your thoughts with this Dakin chap?'

'No, not yet. I wanted to see what you thought first. And, to be honest, I don't really want to get involved unless I'm forced to. I've got more than enough on my plate as it is.'

'Then let me deal with it,' suggested Elliott, his eyes opening wider with excitement at the prospect.

Tom waved his hand. 'Oh no. I'm held in total confidence, remember!'

'A slight impediment, granted, but nothing we can't work round,' batted back Elliott. Already he was beginning to march up and down as he marshalled his thoughts, and, just as when he was at home in his own study, he kept turning like a soldier as he reached the edge of the rug. 'Now, if I sit down with this Dakin —'

'No! Robert! This one you'll have to help with from afar.'

Despite being assertive, Tom suspected his insistence that his friend should remain in the background would be conveniently ignored.

~~~

Green rubbed his bleary eyes and glanced over to the clock positioned on a chest of drawers. He strained to see the
~~~

time. No, that can't be right, he thought and focused on the timepiece even harder. Things started, finally, to come into focus; but the time still read just gone eight o'clock in the morning. 'Bloody Hell!' he cried, realising he'd overslept by over two hours. He threw back his blankets, and lifted himself up, only to fall back exhausted. In total, he reckoned he might have managed a couple of hours sleep. His throbbing head confirmed as much.

The doctor hadn't intended staying up into the early hours, but once he'd started to practise his technique, he'd become totally absorbed. Never once in four hours of working had he checked what the time was.

Properly awake, Green went to open the curtains. The daylight flooded into the room and directly on to the large pig's head placed on the table. Although its bone structure remained, it was hard to recognise it as a pig anymore. The skin had been skilfully pulled back and stitched into tubes, whilst flaps of flesh were perfectly cut out ready for grafting. The arrangement of the head now accurately reflected the painting laid out next to it. Everything had been done exactly as Raven had been teaching him. He gave himself a wry smile in the mirror, knowing his mentor would be impressed with his progress. The night without sleep had been worth it, even if Tom wouldn't be impressed at him being late for his shift.

Across the corridor was Maude's bedroom. He gave a

gentle tap on her door and entered. Much to his relief, he found his younger sister was still fast asleep. Lately the girl had been suffering more than usual with the injuries she'd endured in the fire, which often made her unable to sleep. It pained Green to see Maude in such distress. For all the brutality and suffering he was capable of inflicting on people, he couldn't bear to see his once beautiful sister having to endure pain, sorrow and anxiety. Gently he stroked back her hair and tenderly kissed her forehead. 'Soon, dear sister, very soon. I promise,' he whispered.

Seeing Green in this caring and compassionate role, nobody would have believed he was the same man who had tortured someone to death weeks earlier. The young surgeon, though, had an extraordinary ability to justify his evil behaviour as being totally necessary.

~~~

Checking the clock in his office, Tom wondered if it was beginning to run slow. He checked it once more against his pocket watch, but everything appeared to match. Both timepieces showed twelve minutes past eight. It puzzled Tom that his assistant was not yet on duty. In the six months that Nathan Green had been working for him, never had he been late for his shift. More annoying was that Tom had made an appointment for this morning to
~~~

cross the city and visit Dakin at his offices. But without his junior consultant on hand, he would be forced to cancel. No sooner had he picked up the telephone earpiece than Sister Lucas knocked on his door and entered.

'Sorry to interrupt you, Mr Sharpe, but I've a message from Mr Green.'

The sister spoke clearly and to the point. All around her was the fragrant smell of lavender, which emanated from a pocket full of seeds she would use to help calm anxious patients.

'Good Morning, Sister Lucas,' responded Tom, putting the earpiece back on its stand and smiling broadly. 'Don't tell me … Mr Green has decided to elope with Nurse Brown and sadly, therefore, they won't be in today. In fact, they won't be in ever again!'

'Huh!' Sister Lucas shrugged. 'We should be so lucky, professor,' she continued, confirming that she didn't have many positive feelings about either member of staff.

Tom laughed. He really liked the sister and got on well with her. Despite her outwardly stern appearance, which he was convinced the board of governors made a pre-requisite when recruiting, she was witty, dedicated and always willing to help him. Without her organisational skill, it was doubtful whether Tom would have a clue which theatre he was performing surgery in, or indeed on whom.

Sister Lucas smiled back. 'I'm to inform you that Mr Green rang earlier to advise us that he's been delayed at the station because of a crisis. He'll be in as soon as he's able.'

Although curious as to what the crisis might be, Tom was relieved that his assistant would at least be coming in. Thanking the sister, he went to pick up the patient files on his desk, which seemed fewer than usual. 'Looks like I'm in for a quiet day,' he said optimistically.

'You did ask me yesterday not to schedule you until 1 o'clock today, Mr Sharpe. Remember?'

'Of course I remember,' replied Tom with a smirk.

He held open his door for the sister, but no sooner had she walked a few paces down the corridor, than he called her back into his office and asked her to help with something else. She listened curiously to his request, eventually passing the comment, 'Of course I'll be able to check the theatre registers and ward records, Mr Sharpe, but I can't honestly see them showing Mr Green treating any children. Why would they? He's not a paediatrician.'

'Perhaps he was called in an emergency?' suggested Tom. He was really clutching at straws, but had to be scrupulously fair in his assessment of the situation.

'But you would have known about that, surely, Mr Sharpe?'

When the sister returned later that day with her findings, not surprisingly, she reported that Green hadn't treated or consulted on a child during the preceding three months.

The information merely confirmed to Tom that Elliott was justified in his suspicions of Nathan Green. He gazed out of his window onto the courtyard below, his expression one of deep thought. Whilst he had never felt one hundred per cent sure about Green, he hadn't had him down as a liar. 'Well done, Elliott, old chap,' he said to himself and started to consider further possible motives for Green's behaviour. As he withdrew his gaze from the courtyard, it occurred to him that he was getting the same buzz of excitement from helping Elliott solve his mysteries as he did when performing surgery.

Chapter 12

On turning the corner into the long corridor, all Tom could hear was the loud chatter of typewriters coming from what seemed endless offices, each one with its door wedged open, allowing streams of sunlight to spill across the wooden floor and create shadow entrances on the wall opposite. He could hear the women secretaries' laughter amid the frantic slamming of carriage returns and the continual ringing of bells. Occasionally he stopped and checked for a number on the plain grey doors, which brought a round of flirtatious comments from within. Even for a man used to working with lively women, he couldn't help but feel slightly intimidated.

At a desk by the door of Room 47 a large woman moved her shoulders suggestively, asking, 'And what can you do for me, sweetheart?'

'Phyllis!' interrupted the senior secretary, Emily Dewhirst. 'I'm sorry, sir. How can we help you?'

'Oh yes, thank you. I was …' started Tom, but he was finding it difficult not to be distracted by Phyllis, who was making it obvious her huge breasts were acting as cushions to her wrists as she typed.

'Yes, sorry,' he said, getting back his thread. 'I was looking for Mr Dakin's office. It's Tom Sharpe from St Thomas's Hospital. I have an appointment at half past eleven.'

Emily left him at the mercy of four other secretaries in the room whilst she went to inform Dakin. Once they knew he was a doctor and not someone important from the War Office, the women's innuendo was relentless. Luckily, Tom could give as good as he got, and by the time Emily had returned, he was happily batting playful banter back and forth.

'If you'd like to follow me, Mr Sharpe, I will show you to Mr Dakin's office,' said Emily, her trim frame slightly obscured in a shaft of bright sunlight.

Tom tilted his head. 'My pleasure. Ladies.'

Once he was out of the office, there was a wail of 'Ooh, I do feel faint. Quick, fetch me a doctor!' followed by a chorus of laughter.

'You will have to excuse them, Mr Sharpe,' said Emily, embarrassed at her colleagues insistent teasing.

Tom just gave her an understanding smile. 'Don't worry. It's fine.' Really he was quite flattered.

Once inside Dakin's office it was a more sober affair. Some might even say sombre, because the room looked as inviting as a morgue. The office, which in a previous life had been a bedroom, had on one side a cast-iron fireplace surrounded by a dirty, sage-coloured chimney breast, while on the other wall there was nothing apart from a shabby brown-painted wooden sash window, now with a grill over it. Tom had seen some depressing rooms in his time, but this one had to be one of the worst. Still, this didn't appear to bother its occupant, who was sitting on a rickety cane chair drawn up to a disgustingly filthy desk with a battered filing cabinet to one side of it. Everything stood on a sorry-looking square of threadbare carpet. From the ceiling drooped a makeshift extension to the light pendant, and at the end of the cable, positioned about a yard above Dakin's head, was a converted hanging gas lamp fitted with a drab electric bulb. It really was an awful place to have to work in. Tom doubted anyone would want to visit unless required to do so.

It all suited Dakin, though. He viewed it as ideal, for the simple reason that he was able to lay out all his maps and case files without having to put them away at the end of the day. More importantly, by keeping it cold, dreary and uninviting, he knew no one would want to share the place with him.

Emily made her introduction as quickly as she could, leaving Tom standing just inside the door trying to think of something complimentary to say. Luckily, he didn't have to bother.

'I know what you're thinking, Mr Sharpe, but it's functional and suits my needs,' Dakin declared, continuing to write on his pad. Eventually he looked up. 'Your message was most interesting.' He then rose to his feet, swinging out his chair and offering it to Tom, 'Please.'

Reluctantly Tom accepted and sat down nervously, leaving Dakin to wander round the bleak office, his boots striking loudly on the wooden floor. 'So, you have something that you think may be of interest and could further my investigation, Mr Sharpe?'

'Yes.' Tom opened his jacket and took out the same piece of paper that he'd shown Elliott and placed it on the table. 'It's only a theory you understand.'

'Of course,' said Dakin, picking up the paper and casting his eyes left and right to try and make sense of what he was looking at. An insufferable grin spread across his face. 'They're lines, Mr Sharpe.' His expression began to turn sour. 'Are they supposed to mean something to me?'

Taking back the paper, Tom started to explain all about Daniel, his reaction to the paintings and what he felt it all meant. It wasn't long before Dakin was listening intently. At the mention of interpreting a code, his eyes opened wide, then wider still as Tom reached his conclusion.

Yes, it's feasible, more than feasible, Dakin thought, moving to the window and pinching his forefinger and thumb together on his chin. A few moments later, he'd decided the whole thing needed to be presented to the boffins, as he called them – the men who analysed codes day in and day out. But Dakin realised, just as Tom and Elliott had done, that it was all very well having lines which represented a code, but it still begged the question: how, where and by whom were they being hidden in the picture?

'And that's the bit which, as yet, I haven't been able to understand.'

Dakin seemed somewhat surprised at Tom's comment. 'Well, that's easily rectified. To make sense of it all, we just bring the boy in and make him tell us how it's been done.'

'Make him tell us!' repeated Tom. 'And what exactly does that mean?'

The look on Dakin's face was enough to show he wasn't going to give an honest answer.

'If the lad knows something then we need to interro …'

He paused, realising he ought to change the word, 'Question him, Mr Sharpe.'

'Have you forgotten? I said Daniel is feeble-minded. In fact, in my opinion, he has multiple mental problems.'

'No, I haven't forgotten. They're convenient words we're hearing being used more and more these days.' He gave an unsympathetic snarl, 'Particularly by my colleagues in the conscription office it seems.'

Tom could handle glib comments – he certainly handed out enough of them himself – but there was something about the way Dakin delivered his that really irritated him.

'You speak with such natural, offhand ease, Dakin …'

Tom's deliberate omission of a salutation and the harshness of tone took Dakin aback.

'… Let me assure you, I won't stand by and allow you to treat Daniel like a wooden toy that can be misused until it eventually breaks.'

A truce was needed.

Of course, the intelligence officer didn't care one bit about people's feelings or whether his practices were ethical or not. The reality was that he always did whatever it took to get results, and speaking to Daniel would be no exception. He was smart enough, however, to realise that Tom could prove to be troublesome if he continued to try and ride roughshod over the surgeon's opinions.

Tapping the tip of his cigarette endlessly, Dakin eventually put it in his mouth and struck a match across the rough texture of the exposed plaster on the wall. 'Perhaps we've brought out the worst of each other so far, Mr Sharpe? Be assured I've only got the interests of our noble country at heart, as I'm sure is the case with you.' He inhaled deeply and flicked the discarded match into the unused fireplace. 'Shall we start again and come to a compromise?' he asked, exhaling smoke in time to his words.

Tom was also wise enough to know that playing tit-for-tat with Dakin was fruitless. 'Very well. I will bring Daniel in, but on the strict understanding that I lead and ask the questions – my way!'

'Agreed.'

Tom could have stayed longer and mentioned a possible connection between Daniel and Nathan Green, but at this stage he felt everything was just pure conjecture. He certainly didn't want Dakin going off on a whim, pursuing, or worse arresting, his junior colleague over behaviour that could prove totally innocent.

But Dakin already had Green within his sights.

~~~

The sound of a young woman singing happily and skipping down the stairs above him slowly began to drown out the sound of Tom's own footsteps. Cheerfully swinging her bag in a world of her own, Emily Dewhirst rounded the landing of the stairway and almost collided with him.

'Oooh!' she gasped in shock. 'Do please forgive me, I'm — Oh, it's you, sir. I really am sorry. My mind was somewhere else entirely.'
~~~

'So I could see,' laughed Tom, stepping aside. He swept out his hand, 'Well, don't let me stop you … Whatever it is, it looks as if it's got you excited?'

'I should say it has, Mr Sharpe.' Emily skipped down a couple more steps holding her left hand up high, 'I'm meeting my fiancé for coffee – and to look at rings!' With that she descended to the building's lobby and eventually disappeared through the double doors.

Within five minutes she was standing outside the small temperance coffeehouse, impatiently bouncing her bag against her legs, waiting for her intended, Matthew, to arrive. Emily had arranged specially to take the afternoon off so the pair could finalise the arranging of their wedding, hastily planned for Saturday. Beyond this, there would be no more time – her fiancé was required back on duty at the Front the following Monday.

Sipping her coffee, she asked Matthew, 'These rings from your brother. Everything is definitely above board, isn't it?'

'Of course!' he replied, trying to sound as convincing as possible. The trouble was, he knew his dubious brother only too well. But if he wanted beautiful rings for his bride, then he had little alternative other than to turn a blind eye to his sibling's possible scam.

Several years earlier, the brother, a repair specialist in a firm of prestigious Hatton Garden jewellers, had been found guilty as 'the man on the inside' of a diamond robbery, and had been sentenced to a term of hard labour. Always defiant, his only words in his defence were: 'Desperate times call for desperate measures.'

Eighteen months on, he was back repairing jewellery, this time working for Jenkin and White, Jewellers of Bond Street. His new employment was courtesy of the new skills he'd acquired during his time in prison: enabling him to forge papers and create a whole new identity and background for himself. Now his motto was 'Uncertain times call for creative thinking' – something he practiced in abundance in his new position.

What Emily thought was merely a case of getting a massively discounted price on a damaged, pawned ring that had now been fully restored was, in fact, a racket her future brother-in-law, Reggie, was working to great effect. Using a client's ring that had been brought in for cleaning, he would skilfully create a cheap but totally convincing replica, and would then make the swap when the original was called for. Most often, he would just sell on the original, usually in some back street pub; however, occasionally he got lucky and was able to sell the original numerous times. This he did by offering to resize the ring free of charge, so that it would fit the lady's finger perfectly. Once the deal had been sealed, he'd take back the ring and would be ready to swap it again at his leisure

– a perfectly worked-out swindle that was earning him very good money.

That afternoon, Emily was in for an extra surprise: not only was she viewing her wedding ring, but also an engagement ring.

Chapter 13

Unlike other agents, who quickly learned to silence whatever conscience they might have had, Wilson was always wrestling with his. Since the earliest days of his recruitment, he'd grappled with the fact that what he was doing would ultimately cause the death of innocent people. In those early days, he was heavily influenced by his student friend, Ingrid Schroeder, and held firm to the belief that his activities would bring him retribution for his family's sufferings in South Africa; and for a time, he was able to hold to that view. But now, by working in the hospital, he was constantly reminded of the damage and misery caused by his actions. He had started to question his convictions.

The final straw for the artist came when he had to watch Green tie Beatson to a chair and torture him to death. And things were made decidedly worse when it became obvious that he was under surveillance. Wilson decided he needed to get out. The only problem in getting out, however, was that it was never an option. At the very best, the troubled agent might be able to hedge his bets for the future. Finally, he decided that future would be in England.

Wilson was no fool. His by-now-considerable experience of espionage showed him that the only real way out was to offer himself as a double agent. After that, he could start to devise a way to disappear when the war ended. Such an action could be a risky business. He knew that as soon as he made contact with the British Secret Intelligence Service he might simply be arrested and charged; but he was convinced his intimate involvement with, and knowledge of, the coded drawings could ultimately save him. All the same, Wilson needed to use all the astuteness he was capable of, and for several weeks he carefully plotted a course that would bring him into contact with his German master, Steinhauer's, equivalent in the British War Office. He posted the British officer a series of letters, each one containing just enough information to keep him sufficiently interested to maintain a dialogue. Eventually, Wilson felt confident that he was being taken seriously and broke his cover, agreeing to meet a senior MO5(g) officer, Colonel Coniston.

Two days later, Wilson received the confirmation he needed. Placing a finger between the two net curtains, he made just enough of an opening to enable him to see down to the alley behind the house. What he expected to see was a worker busy pointing the wall with cement, although not for one moment did Wilson believe that was the man's real job. He knew it was much more likely that he was one of Dakin's men, sent to observe him and the building. This morning, however, the worker wasn't there; or that's how it appeared from the little he could see through the narrow gap. He parted the curtains further, only to confirm the man had definitely gone.

Wilson smiled. Looks promising, he thought.

Stepping over discarded clothes strewn on the floor, he made his way to the room at the front of the house. There, he also made a gap in the net curtains and peeped through, this time down towards the newspaper stand on the corner of South Lambeth Road. For two weeks it had been usual to see a look-out pretending to be flicking through the papers. But today, just as at the rear of the house, there was nobody there.

Wilson smiled once more, this time muttering, 'Looks very promising indeed.'

By seven o'clock he was washed, dressed and heading over to the news stand. He purchased his usual copy of the Daily Express and stood studying each page carefully until, eventually, he stopped at what he wanted to see: an illustrated advertisement for Lea & Perrins Worcestershire Sauce, although, on this version, Worchestershire was misspelled with the addition of an 'h'.

Wilson's smile became a massive grin – it was the

acceptance he'd been hoping for. Now he could relax just a little bit more. Unfortunately though, the new double agent had not anticipated the extent to which the tentacles of German espionage had reached into the British war machine. Some much bigger fish than he were working for German masters.

At work that morning, the change in Wilson's demeanour was immediately evident to his colleagues. Even Major Raven couldn't help but pass comment on the man's less tense, more light-hearted manner. At least, that's how it was before Green visited him around two o'clock. The surgeon arrived in the studio in a foul mood after his scheduled surgery sessions with the major. Wilson had never before seen his fellow agent looking so downbeat or so outwardly rattled by something. He could only assume there had been a problem in theatre, although he quickly decided that was probably not the case, since Major Raven had appeared his normal self when he had seen him not five minutes earlier.

'We have a problem,' said Green, with a hint of desperation in his voice.

'We or you?' replied Wilson, looking particularly self-satisfied.

Green gave him a grimace. 'Smugness doesn't suit you, Wilson.' He paused for a second, watching the artist's face, which didn't alter. 'What on earth is wrong with you today?' he said, but didn't wait for Wilson to answer. Instead, he carried on, 'Something happened yesterday evening that needs dealing with.'

To Wilson that meant only one thing – somebody was going to be killed.

'Meet me in Raven's office at three o'clock,' insisted Green.

Wilson raised his eyebrows in surprise at the suggestion.

'Don't worry. From half past two, Raven's back in theatre for the rest of the day.'

'But won't it all look a bit odd?' asked Wilson, his cheerful mood having now totally disappeared.

'What is more normal than me, the new surgeon, discussing matters with the department's head artist? Just pull together some paintings and anything else you'll need to make the meeting appear genuine.'

Right on time, Major Raven left for the operating theatres and Wilson began collecting up some pictures. Moments later, with arms full, he set off for the major's office. 'I'm just going to talk to Mr Green. I shouldn't be long,' he casually mentioned to his colleague.

A good fifteen minutes of waiting in Raven's office had passed when, just as he was on the verge of leaving, the door swung open and Green strolled in.

'Huh, finally,' moaned Wilson. 'We said three o'clock.'

'Well, pardon me,' scorned Green, giving a contemptuous look. For the benefit of anyone watching, he wandered round the office, pointing at the various faces in the pictures and pretended to talk about them.

'So! What is it that's so important it can't wait?' Wilson wanted to know.

Green started to explain the situation and his consequent dilemma.

Eventually, Wilson forced an interruption. 'And now you want to kill the boy and this Mrs Sowerby —'

'They'll simply meet with a tragic accident,' Green abruptly corrected him.

'Good God, they didn't even recognise you! Show some mercy, man … You do understand what that word means?'

Turning his head, Green gave a cold, hard stare. 'It will get done!'

Of that Wilson had no doubt. Irritated, he shook his head. 'How?' he asked.

Green began divulging his plan, which was both daring and brutal.

Undoubtedly Nathan Green was an agent capable of carrying out the most awful, and the most complex tasks if required to do so. In fact, two years earlier he had been judged just the type of person needed by a new German espionage project simply named Tb. This initiative followed the disastrous performance of the 'Nachrichten-Abteilung' intelligence plan, a programme which had all but collapsed when war broke out and most German agents were systematically rounded up and detained by Dakin's war office department, MO5(g).

As head of the British section of the German Admiralty's intelligence service, Steinhauer had to explain the obliteration of his spy network to the Kaiser.

Despite feeling the full onslaught of the emperor's fury, the spymaster was spared an embarrassing dismissal and actually went on to implement project Tb, or 'Hauptberichterstatter T311b' as it was officially titled – a mission aimed at getting 'main corresponder' agents into positions of influence throughout Britain's institutions. From hospitals, universities and government departments, through to the judiciary, achieving infiltration was their highest objective.

By the end of 1915, Green was proving to be a most valuable member of the new programme. Once secure in his junior surgeon position at King George Military Hospital, he set up an effective system for passing secrets back to Germany. It wasn't long before his talents were being further utilised and he was instructed to carry out an assignment to help penetrate the judicial system.

~~~

Visiting Sheffield in the spring of 1916 left Green with two distinct memories – blackened daytime sky and
~~~

the constant smell of sulphur. Both originated from the steelwork furnaces that belched tons of toxic, dirty smoke into the air, and with it an acrid taste that burnt deep into the throat. From his room in a humble bed and breakfast lodging, the young agent looked out onto a blanket of greyness. He just wanted to get on with the task, and then be able to return to London. Pulling his shirt from the hanger in the wardrobe, he found it had an unpleasant smell of rotting eggs. As much as he didn't want to, he really had no alternative but to put it on. He did so with a grimace.

Once outside the city centre, Green, accompanied by a man he referred to as Mr Bywater, could at last get fresh air into his lungs and clothes. In fact, as they approached Judge Sanderson's home, both men were quite surprised at just how much the air quality and scenery had changed for the better in such a short distance.

To Mrs Sowerby, it had appeared to be nothing more than a gas company engineer calling at the door. In reality, it was a very carefully planned tactic to distract her. Wearing overalls, and heavily disguised with a convincing false moustache and beard, Green greeted the housekeeper and notified her that he was required to check households for reported high levels of monoxide in the gas supply. Not suspicious in any way, Mrs Sowerby welcomed him into the house and watched as he held up a strip of thin paper to the ceiling gas lamps in each room. Playing his role of an engineer to perfection, Green then began analysing the resulting colour change. Little did Mrs Sowerby know that all he was doing was singeing the paper. After ten minutes of Green checking and carrying out tests downstairs, she felt he was making a perfectly reasonable request when he asked to be shown to the upper rooms.

Eventually they opened the door into the room occupied by the person Green wanted to see.

'This gentleman is checking our gas lamps, Daniel. He just needs to look at your room,' said Mrs Sowerby.

Daniel didn't look up, and gave no indication of whether he'd even heard, let alone understood. He casually carried on playing.

'What has the man come to do, Daniel?' Mrs Sowerby put her question to the boy a second and third time. After the third prompting, the boy stopped his play and looked up.

'Come to check the lamps,' he said, unperturbed.

Having now located the boy, Green immediately swung into action with the next phase of the plan.

'Well, everything appears in order here, ma'am. If I could just check the meter, then I can be on my way.'

Relieved, Mrs Sowerby was more than willing to oblige. She took him down to the kitchen and pointed to the scullery. 'In there,' she confirmed.

Using more of his cunning, Green kept the housekeeper in the scullery long enough to allow him to let Bywater into the house. 'If you could just watch this top dial for me, ma'am,' he stated and moved towards the hall. 'Let me know if it moves to number 2 when I increase the pressure in a few lamps.'

Once in the house and directed to Daniel's room, Bywater wasted no time in striding upstairs to carry out Green's instructions. Standing outside the bedroom, he opened a small medicine bottle and tipped the chloroform-based mixture onto a thick wad of cotton gauze. Carefully he turned the door handle and gently pushed.

Daniel never even noticed the door open. He was far too busy throwing his soldiers about. 'Bang! Bosch!' he cried, as they all collided into a heap. Suddenly, everything went silent and black. The boy slumped unconscious onto his imaginary battlefield, and seconds later, Bywater was dragging the limp body towards the stairs.

Chapter 14

Their meeting had been arranged for one o'clock and by five past the hour Green and Bywater were seated in the judge's study, engaged in what appeared to be polite, businesslike conversation. By the time the large, ornate grandfather clock struck the half hour, however, the men were all standing and talking in an aggressive manner.

Convening at the judge's house had been the owner's suggestion. Any person who might help the Asylum Trust, of which he was a trustee, and for which he worked tirelessly, was welcome in Judge Sanderson's home. Mrs Sowerby, though, felt that most visitors were there simply as salesmen for pharmaceutical companies, wanting to persuade the judge to use his influence to get hospitals to trial their drugs. Judge Sanderson knew that his housekeeper's opinion was, sadly, invariably the truth, although he was far too honourable to allow his position in the judiciary to be compromised. That was until today.

Using the pseudonym of Nigel Shelton, Green and his colleague, who called himself Sydney Bywater, were visiting the judge in the guise of directors of a company manufacturing silver plated cutlery. They had indicated their company's willingness to offer a sizable donation to the Trust. The reason given was Mr Bywater's desire to repay the Asylum for the kindness afforded his late brother during his institutionalisation.

As quickly as the conversation had started, it stopped. 'I'm sorry?' said the judge, confused. Had he heard the man correctly?

Bywater twisted his head round slightly and gave a wry smile. 'I said, now to the real reason why we're here.'

Still the judge looked confused, but slowly the situation became obvious. He was being tricked.

'A heart rendering story, I'm sure you'll agree,' added Bywater.

Judge Sanderson rose from his seat, enraged at their cunning, 'How dare you!' he barked, his face reddening. 'Get out! Get out of my house immediately!'

'Without hearing our requirements? That's most uncharitable, sir.'

'Out! Out!'

The judge waved his arms furiously, trying to propel them out. A hand came up and pushed hard onto his chest.

'Why don't you just calm down, sir, and listen very carefully to what we have to say,' advised Green.

'This is preposterous! Two men entering my property,

telling me …' He stopped himself, wondering why he was even attempting further conversation. Reaching out he picked up the phone on his desk. 'Shelton and Bywater wasn't it?'

Green encouraged the judge to make his call. Sanderson snapped his fingers down on the bar and tapped it repeatedly, squawking, 'Hello! Hello! Operator! Hello!'

There was no response.

'Do you honestly think we'd leave the telephone working?'

'Who exactly are you?' the judge said, slowly replacing the earpiece.

Lifting his head, he saw the gun suddenly pointing directly at him, its barrel moving closer and closer to his head. Over the years, he had dealt with many awkward situations, but never in his life had he faced anything as serious as this. Who were these two men threatening him in his own house? What did they really want?

The cold metal of the gun finally touched his forehead.

'If it's money, I don't keep any in the house,' the judge muttered, now convinced that he was the victim of a very elaborate and frightening burglary.

He was surprised by Green's response. 'Very wise of you, sir.'

There was a brief silence before he heard the awful sound of the gun being cocked, the click of the hammer booming loud in his head. He wanted to remain calm and negotiate, but his mouth was so dry it made speaking difficult. Eventually, he managed to swallow.

'If it's not money, then I don't understand.'

Really though, the judge ought to have understood. During his career, there had been any number of people whom he'd sent to the cells, and who might now want to get even in some way.

The barrel moved away unexpectedly. 'I shan't kill you,' declared Green, dropping his arm.

Sanderson breathed a deep sigh of relief.

'Unless, of course, you decide not to co-operate.'

Gathering his composure, the judge frowned. 'Co-operate?'

His query brought a snigger from Green before he spoke. 'You see, our dear Mr Lloyd George and his new cabinet want us to believe Britain can win this war ...' He paused and began to study the carriage clock on the mantelpiece. He moved it slightly to the left in order to centre it, before carrying on talking. 'I ask you, what stupidity! We all know Germany has and always will have the upper hand. But alas, there's nothing more satisfying than watching the rats of a country eating from the hand that's laid a trap for them.'

Sanderson looked bemused. Were the men actually nothing more than a pair of political activists, he wondered.

'Do you not follow?' enquired Green, sarcastically. 'It's quite easy. You're going to be one of the people helping us lay that trap.'

The judge, at last, understood the man's inference. 'You want me to compromise my country in some way!' he gasped with incredulity.

A grin spread across Green's face as he slowly began clapping. 'Well done. Well done indeed.' Moving in closer to the judge, he glared down on him menacingly and declared, 'Yes, that's exactly what you're going to do.'

Had it not been for the fact that he was being held at gun point, Sanderson might have let out a really raucous laugh. As it was, he resisted the temptation and instead just adopted a contemptuous tone of voice. 'Please do tell me more,' he said. 'For example, how on earth you're going to get one of the most prominent judges on the northern court circuit to work against his country?' He looked again at the gun still pointing at him. 'And do correct me if I'm wrong, but if you shoot me, I become of no further use to you.'

Green was happy to play the game, at least for a little while longer and un-cocked the gun.

'Yes, I must admit, I had to ask that same question. But then, I was reminded … blood is thicker than water.'

Sanderson's look of contempt immediately turned to one of anger when his captor took out his pocket watch, checked the time and spoke to his colleague. 'It won't be long now before Daniel comes round, Mr Bywater. He is securely bound, isn't he?'

'Oh indeed,' replied Bywater, in a sinister voice.

Horrified, the judge looked up and stared at each man in turn. 'Where is he? Where is my son?' he demanded to know; but neither Bywater nor Green gave him an answer. 'If anything has happened to my son,' hissed Sanderson, attempting to rise from his chair, only to be pushed back down firmly.

Green spoke calmly, 'You do have a choice, Judge. No harm will come to Daniel, providing you follow my instructions to the letter.'

The judge reacted just as he would have in court, and threw out the suggestion immediately. 'Let's get one thing clear! I will not be threatened or blackmailed by you or anyone.'

Bywater saw the nod from his colleague and threw him a cushion. Green placed it against the judge's heart and leant forward to whisper, 'Now, let me make one thing clear to you.' Pulling back the hammer, he re-cocked his gun and pushed the barrel deep into the feather filled cushion. 'You have precisely ten seconds,' he explained calmly. 'Decide! Either the boy still has a father, albeit one with principles slightly tarnished; or here lie a patriotic father and son. Both died so needlessly!'

A chilling smile spread across his face, 'Oh, and trust me, judge. Daniel will be killed. One … two … three …'

Never before had the judge been on the brink of such a devastating choice. He closed his eyes.

'Seven … eight.' The gun pushed harder into the cushion. 'Nine.'

'All right! All right!'

The judge turned his panic stricken eyes towards his tormentor. 'All right. But first I want to see Daniel.'

~~~

The three men walked in silence down the curved driveway towards the road, only the crunch of gravel beneath their feet breaking into the tense silence. Eventually, they stopped at the back of a transport wagon. Bywater reached out towards the canvas panel and pulled it up to reveal piles of boxes, with a mound of tarpaulin to one side of them. He climbed carefully into the wagon and lifted the sheeting. Underneath lay Daniel – out cold.

Judge Sanderson dropped his head, defeated. 'Show me he's still alive, at least,' he begged.

Bywater waited for a nod from his colleague before producing a small bottle, which he opened and passed under Daniel's nostrils. It was enough to ensure the boy began stirring. That was, until the gauze was again gently laid across the boy's nose, and he once more fell unconscious.

'Evil, heartless swine!' the judge cried, despising the
~~~

men and the whole affair.

'10 o'clock,' was all that Green replied, showing no hint of compassion.

The cryptic comment referred to the time that the judge should appear from inside the city library building and look up and down the street three times. It was part of a plan which, if he followed it precisely, would ensure the safe return of Daniel.

Judge Sanderson had for several years been a non-executive director of a company of steelmakers, and a founder member of a new wartime committee formed to co-ordinate Sheffield's massive munitions production effort. All members of this committee were privy to lots of secret technical drawings of military hardware; drawings that Sanderson was tasked to temporarily remove from the site so they could be photographed.

As instructed, at a quarter past nine the next morning the judge entered the city library. With a large roll of paper under his arm, he made his way up the stairs to the third level and went to sit in a brown leather tub chair. He had been told to read the Daily Mirror newspaper there until a quarter to ten, at which time, he should lay out the paper on the reading table and place a single drawing against each of pages 4, 8 and 12. On closing the newspaper, he was to proceed down to the entrance and wait until exactly 10 o'clock, before going outside to look up and down the street. Only after doing all this, could he return and retrieve the drawings.

In the space of just two short days, a fine, hitherto outstanding, judge had turned into a desperate man, forced into assisting the enemy in industrial espionage, the enormity of which Spymaster Steinhauer could only have dreamed.

Judge Sanderson also realised that carrying out a plan like this only the once would never be an option.

Chapter 15

'Is she being naughty again?' asked Daniel, watching at the door. The question took Mary by surprise. She thought briefly how best to answer. How do you tastefully explain the reasons for changing a nappy?

'No, it's just she needs changing and doesn't like it,' she eventually replied, deciding no more detail was needed.

The conversation was interrupted by Mrs Sowerby calling out Daniel's name. Arriving at the doorway, she quickly realised the boy was intruding and insisted, 'Come along now, Daniel. Let's leave Mrs Sharpe to deal with baby Lucinda. You can help me write these postcards.'

'It's all right, Mrs Sowerby, I don't mind,' interrupted Mary, although seeing the woman raise her eyebrows, she felt she ought to reaffirm her ease with the situation. 'Really, I don't mind … So, how were things on your visit to the city?'

For the next five minutes, Mary listened to Daniel excitedly explaining all about the famous landmarks they had seen. She smiled. It was lovely to see him so content and happy.

'Oh, before I forget, Mrs Sharpe,' said Mrs Sowerby, looking into her bag to find the jewellery envelope, 'I picked up your rings as requested.'

Gesturing that she was a little too pre-occupied to try them on, Mary asked Daniel to take the envelope for her and leave it on the dressing table. He did so but couldn't resist trying to undo the seal and check the contents.

Mrs Sowerby speedily moved to stop him. 'No, Daniel! It's what we collected from the jewellery shop earlier and it belongs to Mrs Sharpe. So it's not our business. Remember?'

Daniel had clearly forgotten the conversation but accepted the explanation and put the envelope on the dressing table. However, it was obvious that he was still curious.

Offering a distraction, Mary asked, 'Perhaps, Daniel, you'd like to come with Lucinda, Mrs Elliott and me when we go to the park tomorrow?'

She looked over to Mrs Sowerby to add, 'Mr Sharpe and Mr Elliott are going into the city, so you can have the day totally alone.'

The new housekeeper couldn't deny the idea sounded very appealing, but Daniel just shook his head adamantly.

'That's very kind of you, Mrs Sharpe.' She stroked Daniel's hair to one side. 'We'll have a chat about it, eh.'

~~~
~~~

It was the Elliott's last full day of staying with the Sharpes in London, and unfortunately Tom had to work. Ann had anticipated that her husband would baulk at spending the day in the park, so suggested he might want to travel into the city with Tom and then look up an old acquaintance whom he'd first met at a court probationers' conference.

Elliott and the London Underground were not a very harmonious combination. The Yorkshireman disliked travelling on all forms of public transport, instead preferring to walk to places whenever possible. However, he knew that just wasn't feasible in London and, as the tube train emerged from the dark tunnel, he resigned himself to the next experience of being jostled and squeezed mercilessly into a carriage. Even though he had visited London on numerous occasions, Elliott couldn't ever remember it being as busy as this morning. To make matters worse, because of his accent, everyone he spoke to seemed to ask him to repeat himself, believing he was a foreigner. After an hour of travelling, he was convinced most Londoners needed to have their ears syringed.

Tom smiled, as he always did when watching his friend become agitated over the most trivial things; but he'd known Elliott long enough to realise that in these situations it was best to just leave him to his own devices. Eventually, he'd come round and accept the situation.

'Don't forget, up Long Acre and right into Bow Street,'

shouted Tom, giving a wry smile to his friend as he got out of the carriage and the doors closed. He knew full well what was coming. As the train pulled away, Elliott's heart sank at seeing the sign:

LIFTS CLOSED FOR REPAIRS

Only gradually did he realise this meant passengers having to tackle a winding staircase of 193 steps. Even for a relatively fit man like Elliott, the climb was exhausting. At last, he trudged up the final few steps and rested.

'Ah, young man,' he called breathlessly to a passing attendant, 'Which way for Long Acre?'

The attendant hadn't understood a word, and so pulled out his pocket watch and gave his standard response about the tourist omnibus. 'At half past the hour, sir. Right outside here … Next one due any minute now. Which country you from then, sir?'

Elliott shook his head in utter frustration. Pulling himself up and standing tall, he gave his sarcastic reply, 'The Federal Republic of the West Riding.'

Sufficiently recovered, Elliott set off again, although he hadn't walked more than two hundred yards up Long Acre when he heard the drone of engines high above in the sky. Like everybody else, he looked upwards and could make out the shapes of about a dozen aircraft. One man near him began cheering and clapping, thinking it was the return of a British patrol. Soon, a crowd had gathered and joined in the patriotic celebration. A string of white flashes flying up into the sky, followed by the bark of anti-aircraft guns, instantly stopped the cheering. People continued to stare upwards, astonished that they were under attack from enemy aircraft in broad daylight. Few took immediate cover.

The first bomb descended on the dockyards to the east with a deafening screech. But then, a ferocious explosion ripped through some nearby buildings with devastating ease. Elliott cowered on the ground at the subsequent loud thuds and resulting massive balls of fire and smoke that filled the sky. It all seemed so near. People appeared too stunned to take cover and just wandered around. Only when the air raid siren started up, giving its distinct whirring noise, did they begin to react.

Within minutes, the sound of a continuous whistle could be heard in the distance. Elliott knew instantly it was that of a policeman. Sure enough, towards him came a constable peddling his bicycle for dear life and blowing furiously, with a placard around his neck stating 'TAKE COVER'.

Another bomb exploded close by ... and another.

People started to run in all directions, screaming. Chaos reigned.

Yet another incendiary unleashed its carnage.

Elliott knew he needed to double back to the relative safety of the underground station. He gathered speed as smoke began to drift down the street, causing even more mayhem. The shrill note of a little girl's cry, however, forced him to stop and look back.

At first he couldn't see her, only hear her words, 'Mummy! Mummy!'

Then, through the confusion emerged a sobbing infant, her dress covered in blood and dirt.

'Here, sweetheart,' called Elliott, holding out his arms.

The disorientated girl, about four years old, hesitated, her thumb placed firmly in her mouth for comfort. With her other hand she held tightly onto a small knitted doll. Once more, Elliott beckoned her towards him, this time giving a broad reassuring smile. Sniffing away her tears, she pushed out her quivering bottom lip and walked over, crying. 'I've lost my mummy.'

Safe in Elliott's arms, the girl snuggled in deep and stared up at him with tear-filled eyes. She had no real understanding of what was happening, and was bewildered as to why her mother, her world of security, had suddenly disappeared. He parted her tousled, yet still beautiful, silky blonde hair and kissed her head.

'Don't you worry! I'll find your mummy.'

What else could he have said?

The dust was now accumulating so thickly that Elliott

had trouble seeing ten feet in front of him, but he knew he had to go and look for the girl's mother, no matter how much his instinct was telling him it would be futile. Through the corner of his eye a young nurse caught his attention. She had watched the whole incident and offered him a smile. 'Why don't you let me take her to the underground?' she said. 'We'll wait there while you go and take a look for her mother.'

An appreciative Elliott nodded.

The nurse held out her hand to the girl. 'How about we go and take dolly to see the trains?' Unsure, the girl shook her head, but the young nurse persisted. 'It's important we let this gentlemen go and look for mummy.' She stretched out her hand further, beckoning the girl to take hold.

Still petrified, the girl reached out, allowing the nurse to pick her up and hold her tightly.

'My name is Gemma. May I ask your name?'

A shaky little voice replied. 'I'm Esmi.'

'What a lovely name that is.'

Happy that the girl was taken care of, Elliott disappeared up the dust laden street and quickly found it almost impossible to see a thing. He felt his way along the buildings, stumbling over bits of debris strewn across the pavement. Soon, he had trouble negotiating a path – rubble lay everywhere. In the distance he could hear voices which he realised were those of the emergency services.

Almost tripping over something, Elliott pulled up. He looked down to his feet and discovered a body in his way. He bent over and gingerly felt for a pulse, although quite why he did so he wasn't sure: the whole torso was ripped to shreds; surviving such injuries would have been a miracle. A distraught voice broke his concentration.

'My daughter! Have you found my daughter?' screamed the woman at a fireman, assessing her injuries.

'We're doing everything we possibly can to find people, ma'am.'

Elliott staggered over the twisted remains of an office window. 'Your daughter, miss, what's her name?'

The bewildered woman grabbed at his arm, crying, 'You've found her? Arh dear gawd, tell me you've —'

'What's her name, miss?' Elliott insisted.

'Esmi. Her name's Esmi.'

Elliott's sudden smile was enough for the woman to know her daughter was still alive.

'Yes, she's fine, miss. Safe and sound in the underground back there. Come! I'll take you to her.'

She fell into his arms sobbing. 'Thank you, sir. Thank you ever so much.'

Clambering back over the rubble, the couple could begin to see the dust settling ahead of them. Moments later the underground building came into view. But, with a sudden shriek, Elliott pulled up. There was a terrible pain in his leg, and he was unable to move forward. Looking down, the problem was clear: he'd become entangled in a mass of industrial wire. He attempted to release himself by pulling at his trousers, but it wasn't that simple: the more he pulled, the more the razor-sharp wire tore into his leg.

'Here, let me help,' offered the woman, though clearly all she wanted to do was run to the underground and be reunited with her daughter.

Elliott knew as much. Besides which, he'd much rather carefully move the wire himself. 'No, you go on ahead. I can deal with this.'

They were the last words the probation officer said before a ten-pound bomb slammed into the top of the printing works across the road from him. The explosion tore the building apart with staggering power, hurling large printing presses against any outer wall that was left standing. As he felt the force of the blast throwing him hard against the wall, Elliott watched a mass of bricks and debris fly high into the air. Everything went into slow motion as all manner of things began raining down all around him. Instinctively, he covered his head with his arms in an attempt to shield himself. A spinning wooden door suddenly came hurtling towards him. It crashed across his head and shoulders, knocking him to the ground unconscious. Now he was at the mercy of whatever else was left to fall.

~~~

Tom remembered clearly the time the attack started, because he'd just been called to the ward to see a patient suffering complications from surgery. On arrival, he found the man going into cardiac arrest. Ten minutes later, despite his best efforts to revive him, he was certifying the time of death as 11.28am. It was immediately after this that he heard the same drone of aircraft high over London, and watched in horror as the Gotha bombers dropped their terrible cargo on the city.

It wasn't long before the hospital was placed on full alert in expectation of receiving many of the casualties. Every telephone suddenly seemed to be ringing and people were rushing about like worker ants, carrying equipment and wheeling trolleys up and down.

'I do hope you've eaten, Mr Sharpe?' said Sister Lucas, holding out a surgical gown for Tom to push his arms into. 'At least 80 of the injured are being brought to us, apparently.'

'Wonderful!' sighed Tom. 'You'd better contact my wife and tell her I doubt I will be home this evening.' He knew from bitter experience that most of the injured
~~~

would be in need of surgery.

Soon, Tom was taking full control of his department.

'Stop!' he shouted. 'Everyone please stop what you're doing.'

It took a while, but everybody broke off from their tasks and stood quite still. What seconds earlier had been a preparation area of frantic activity was now perfectly calm and quiet. They all waited for Tom to speak.

'Ladies and Gentlemen,' he started. 'Very shortly we will experience probably one of our most challenging days for a long while. I want you to know that there is no other team of talented people that I'd rather be working with right now. May God be with us all!' There was a spontaneous round of applause, which was only broken by the double doors bursting open and orderlies bringing in the first casualties. Everything quickly returned to organised chaos.

Operating continuously on the wounded was grueling, and it was four hours before Tom was finally able to take a short break. Even outside the theatre though, he carried on working by joining the student doctors in a corridor assessing the next batch of injured people.

Assessments fell into three simple categories: 'dying', 'serious' or 'attention'. The dying were taken straight to theatre, whilst the seriously injured were allocated a numbered luggage label which was placed on top of any notes. Orderlies would then tie these labels to the bed frame and move beds around as required. All 'attention' casualties were eventually moved to an appropriate department for treatment.

Tom went down the lines of patients, checking the different assessments. He peered down at the legs of one assessed patient not allocated a numbered label and looked concerned – the left leg was easily two inches shorter than the right. Surely not, he thought and scooped up the case notes. They simply stated 'suspected leg fracture'. Tom flicked over the page expecting to see more, but there was no mention of what he knew was almost certainly a split femur.

'Doctor!' Tom called.

A tired young man pushed back his hair and replied, 'Yes, Mr Sharpe.'

'Who carried out this assessment?'

The doctor took hold of the folder being offered him and studied the notes. He glanced to the patient before acknowledging, 'It was me, sir. Why, is there a problem?'

'Very much so,' replied Tom. He glanced round and called out, 'Ah, nurse. Go and fetch me a Thomas splint immediately please.'

The young doctor began to realise his mistake and dropped his head. 'I'm sorry, Mr Sharpe, I must have —'

'The first thing to check on any leg fracture, doctor,

should be to see if there is a shortening of the leg,' Tom interrupted. He paused and made the student look at him. 'Why is that?'

'Because it might signal a fractured femur, sir?'

'Indeed. And the chances of survival without fitting a Thomas splint?'

'Probably less than twenty per cent,' the doctor conceded, before adding, 'I honestly don't know how I managed to miss it, Mr Sharpe.'

Although the doctor had made a basic error which might have had tragic consequences, Tom wasn't a professor to give a student a stern lecture in front of everyone, unless they deserved it. In this case, he decided he'd discuss the matter further at a more appropriate time. 'More haste, less speed,' he simply reminded the student and pushed the folder onto his chest. 'Straight to theatre with him please.'

Turning his attention to the patient, Tom called, 'Sir … Sir, can you hear me?'

But there was no response.

'… As quickly as you can, doctor. The man is in severe shock.'

Tom began helping to manoeuvre the bed, but suddenly stopped as the patient's dirty, dusty face came clearly into view. 'Dear God!' he cried, realising who it was.

Elliott's gaunt face confirmed he was only just clinging onto life.

Chapter 16

Perhaps it was a sixth sense. Or maybe it was nothing more than a natural reaction to watching the air raid and knowing their loved ones were in the city. Either way, Ann and Mary felt very anxious when the telephone rang that afternoon.

'London 4372,' answered Mary nervously.

'You're connected now, caller,' Tom heard. He cleared his throat. 'Darling, it's me.'

'Tom! Oh, thank goodness you've rung.'

But Mary's expression of joy was quickly replaced by a worried, tense look as she listened more to her husband's words. Before long, she was fighting back the tears, although a series of barely stifled gasps gave the game away. Mary put down the telephone and glanced over to Ann. Unable to stop herself, she burst out crying.

'Mary! What on earth is it? What's wrong?'

Desperately trying to regain her composure and be strong for Ann's sake, Mary wiped away her tears and breathed in deeply. 'It's Robert, he's —'

She didn't have time to say any more. Her friend was

already buckling in front of her, fearing the worst.

'No! No! It's not that.'

As Mary began to explain the situation, Ann's immediate panic subsided; but her heart continued to beat like a hammer striking an anvil. She was overcome with conflicting emotion: anguish that Elliott had been seriously injured in the bombing; joy that he was still alive. She fanned her face, trying to calm herself down further.

Slowly her joy began to turn to exasperation. 'What did I say to him this morning?' she said, holding her hands open. 'Come to the park with me, Robert. Enjoy the fact we're able to spend the day together … What did I get back? … Huh! A look of bewilderment, as if I'd told him there was another child on the way.'

In the end, Ann's dry sense of humour had to surface. As she sat back in her chair, a thought crossed her mind. She bit her bottom lip and smiled. 'Oh Mary, I do hope he had clean long johns on!'

Both women burst out laughing.

'Well, I'd better get across to the hospital. Otherwise, knowing Robert, he'll have decided to discharge himself.'

'I'm coming with you,' insisted Mary.

'But what about Lucinda?'

'We'll take her with us. I might be able to sneak through and let her see Tom. By all accounts, it sounds like he won't be home until much later tonight.'

Tom's swift action, along with a lengthy operation and a degree of luck, meant Elliott wasn't laid out in the hospital mortuary. Instead, he was now lying on a ward in a morphine-induced sleep, with his leg in a cast and held up in traction.

Looking at him, Ann couldn't prevent a lump rising in her throat. She swallowed hard, trying to stop her tears being seen by the other patients. 'Hello husband,' she whispered playfully, taking hold of his hand and kissing it.

A voice from the next bed disturbed her tender moment. 'At least he didn't have to cross the channel to cop for Jerry's lot. Still, a good story to tell the grandchildren in years to come, eh?'

Ann smiled at the thought. She turned to answer the man. 'Only the grandchildren, sir? Now that's wishful thinking!'

Squeezing his hand a little more tightly, she stood for a moment, realising just how much she did love Elliott, despite all his funny little ways. Carefully she placed his hand down by his side and left to meet Tom and Mary.

After sitting down in Tom's office, Ann was told exactly how long the recovery process might be. Although the parts of his bone had been successfully realigned during surgery, the likelihood was that Elliott would be spending at least a week in hospital and six to eight weeks in a plaster cast. Then, if he was lucky, complete rehabilitation would take six months. At worse, it could be a year. Ann wrinkled her nose at the prospect. She knew her husband's impatience only too well. Aiding his physical recovery would be easy compared to handling his inevitable frustration and irritability with the situation.

Finally, Tom suggested she should delay her return to Sheffield for a couple of days in order to ensure there were no major complications. She agreed, and later that evening decided to telephone her parents to explain the crisis and to talk to her children, Henry and Cecil. For the boys, though, even though they were concerned for their father, all it really meant was that they could spend more time sea fishing and playing about in rock pools at Scarborough.

Tom opened his wallet, pulled out a piece of paper and offered it to Ann. 'Here! I've written down the name of an orthopedic surgeon I used to work with in Sheffield. He's good. I'll ask him to keep an eye on Robert.'

'But —' started Ann, worried about fees they couldn't afford.

'You just make the appointment,' interrupted Tom, seeing her obvious concern. 'Let me deal with the rest.'

On closing his wallet, he immediately felt impelled to re-open it and study the contents; but, no matter how many times he looked, everything appeared normal. He knew, though, that something wasn't right. He just couldn't see the obvious difference that was staring him in the face. The tramlines began to appear on his forehead.

'Is everything all right, Tom?' asked Mary.

'Yes. I thought I'd lost a piece of paper. That's all.' He shook his head in confusion and closed his wallet.

A knock on the door interrupted the conversation.

Nathan Green breezed in. 'I was just …' he announced, but immediately paused, on realising his colleague had company. 'I do apologise … Oh, it's you, Mrs Sharpe, hello … and Mrs Elliott. I'm dreadfully sorry about Mr Elliott, ma'am.'

Green had come to collect some x-rays he needed to take back to St Thomas's that afternoon. As usual, Tom wasn't prepared and didn't have a clue where he'd put them. He began foraging through mounds of documents in an attempt to find the folder.

The question of how he could manage to meet Mary again had consumed Green ever since the Sharpe's dinner party. Everything he remembered about her had become etched indelibly on his mind, and now, once again, he struggled to take his eyes off his colleague's wife. Fascination had slowly turned to obsession. He had drifted into fantasy, imagining how it could be. There was nothing about Mary he didn't consider perfect. He adored what he saw, craved every inch of her; every feature, every gesture filled his mind.

Green watched Tom fumbling with a pile of papers. 'Patience, Nathan,' he said to himself, feeling his jealousy well up. He knew he had to temper his frustration, even though his chilling decision had been made. A shout brought an abrupt end to his contemplation. Tom had found the x-rays, although, quite why they were wedged between two screwed-up towels he couldn't think.

It didn't take long for Green to turn his attention to the other matter that was consuming him – Mrs Sowerby and Daniel. He realised that with Elliott on the ward, and the Sharpes and Mrs Elliott also here in the hospital, that left the housekeeper and the boy alone in the house. A situation he thought most fortuitous.

Bidding farewell, he left the office. However, instead of heading straight for the exit, he returned to his own office and reached for the telephone.

~~~

Picking up the photograph that had been put down on the table in front of him, Wilson naturally wondered what Green expected him to do with it. He glanced at the subject, but still remained puzzled. Was it meant to hold some significance for their activities?

Green certainly wasn't very forthcoming. 'Well?' he simply asked.
~~~

'Well what?' Wilson had to concede.

'What do you think?'

Wilson looked once more at the photograph and eventually gave his opinion. 'The composition's good, it's well lit —'

'Idiot!' snapped Green and snatched back the photograph.

'Well bloody hell, Nathan, what do you want me to say?'

Finding some clothes at his feet, Green kicked them against the wall. 'You ought to tidy up this damned hovel,' he hissed, and moved towards the chair, from which he flung a kit bag onto the floor so that he could sit down. 'What I meant was, what do you think of her?'

The photo was gently laid back on the table.

'She's undeniably pretty,' said Wilson, picking up the photo again. 'Yes, she's lovely. But then so are lots of women.'

'I want you to draw and paint her.'

Wilson looked confused. 'What, with code? Why?'

'No!' shouted Green. 'Just a picture, exactly as you see her there.'

It took a moment for Wilson to grasp the fact that Green was actually showing genuine sentiment towards another person. He began to laugh. Could it be that the man he'd only ever known as completely coldblooded had fallen for a woman?

Green wasn't one for being teased, and certainly not

ridiculed; but despite his brutal, aggressive character, he wasn't a big man. Wilson would easily be able to match him in a physical altercation. It was a brave man, however, who would fight Green, because the spy always took his revenge, and his idea of consequences always meant awful suffering. The artist knew that by laughing he was inviting an unpleasant outcome; but equally, he wasn't afraid, as once he might have been. Besides, at this moment he held the trump card – he could draw.

'How long will it take?' asked Green.

Wilson shrugged with indifference. 'A day or so, I suppose.' He studied the photo a little more closely anticipating the amount of work that would be involved. For the first time, he turned it over and saw the message:

TO MY DARLING TOM
LOVE MARY

Only then did it begin to occur to Wilson who the woman might be. He thought back to a time in Tom's office when he had been delivering some drawings. He remembered well that Tom's wallet had been left open on the desk and, as he put the artwork down, he couldn't help but admire the photo. 'My wife, Mary,' he distinctly recalled the professor saying.

'This is —'

'Gorgeous, isn't she,'

'This is Tom Sharpe's wife. Jesus Christ, Nathan, look!' cried Wilson, indicating the back of the photo.

Green gave his smug, omniscient look. 'Yes, I must remember to change that message after I've … Oops! What am I saying, Arthur?'

Wilson stood there dumbfounded. Eventually, he spat out his question. 'You're going to do away with Tom Sharpe, aren't you?'

'Well, I can't have him getting in the way now, can I?' Green replied in a tone of complete indifference.

The fact that Green was serious was never in question. When in pursuit of a particular goal, the doctor found the taking of life merely a necessary activity. The problem for Wilson was understanding his fellow agent's goals. At the beginning, they had always been aligned to Steinhauer's Hauptberichterstatter projects; but now the lines seemed blurred. Green, in his colleague's opinion, was seeking to carry out his own agenda. And with Dakin suddenly making headway in unraveling the whole mission, the last thing needed was Green compromising the master plan through his perverse personal aspirations.

Even if it were made to look like an accident, Wilson knew that arranging for Tom Sharpe to be killed would only raise Dakin's suspicions further, causing him to re-double his efforts in investigating matters. And, with the arrangements the artist had recently concluded, that couldn't be allowed to happen. He needed time to make contact with his spymaster and get some guidance.

In the meantime, Green had already triggered his plan for Mrs Sowerby and Daniel.

At quarter past five that afternoon, Mrs Sowerby was washing some pots when the brass knocker struck the front door!

Chapter 17

Dakin was furious that surveillance on Wilson's home had been pulled without his knowledge. Not since his days in the special branch had he felt so thoroughly frustrated and sidelined. He was determined to find out the truth. In an attempt to discover anything that might incriminate Wilson, he had his whole team of secretaries checking and rechecking records, all of which had to be done in addition to their normal daily duties. It wasn't long before the angry women were being deliberately awkward to frustrate Dakin even further.

Thus when Dakin arrived for an appointment at the fourth floor office of his superior, Colonel Edward Coniston, he was already in a state of agitation. He pulled down his jacket and tried to look as calm as possible; and then he waited … and waited … and waited some more. In fact, Dakin had to kill time for over twenty minutes before being seen. By the time the door was opened by C, as he insisted on being addressed, Dakin was so angry that he would have liked to grab hold of the colonel and thump him.

The conversation proceeded much as Dakin had expected it would. He listened to the often foul-mouthed department head talking about the stupidity of his fellow officers in Whitehall, and then about the awful effect the war was having on supplies of his favourite Riesling. A disillusioned Dakin could certainly agree with the former, but didn't have the slightest interest in the latter. After a fifth rendition of 'It's absolute bollocks, do you hear?' Dakin knew he needed to seize the initiative. That was if he wanted to get back to his office that day.

Dakin cleared his throat with a loud cough, much to the displeasure of the colonel, who hadn't fully finished giving his opinion.

'Sir, if I may bring your attention to the purpose of my visit.'

Reluctantly, Colonel Coniston agreed to change the subject and leant back in his chair. 'Yes, I received your memo,' he said, rolling a pencil between his fingers.

Trying to be as diplomatic as he could, Dakin began his quest for answers, although it wasn't long before he hit a brick wall.

'I gave the order to suspend surveillance,' the colonel interrupted. 'You had men there for three weeks and, as I understand it, they returned nothing of consequence. Resources are scarce.'

'With respect sir, three weeks is hardly a long time when —'

'That's my decision, Dakin.'

A heavy silence descended. Ordinarily, that would have been the end of the meeting; but this time, Dakin decided to speak out whatever the repercussions might be. 'I'm being bloody warned off, aren't I?'

The colonel raised his eyebrows. 'Watch your mouth, Dakin.'

'There was no reason to pull those men just like that.'

'I've told you, resources are scarce and —'

'No! No!' Dakin butted in, determined to have his say. 'You've read my intelligence reports. You know exactly how near we were to unearthing something very substantial.'

'Nobody is suggesting we cease your precious investigation, Dakin, just that we scale back any unnecessary use of men.'

Each man fixed the other with a stare.

Defiant, Dakin gave his parting shot. 'Absolute bollocks, do you hear?' Swinging round, he headed straight for the door before stopping to add, 'Sir!'

He knew his words would almost certainly cost him his position; but he had reached the stage where he didn't care.

The colonel was seething. In his fury, he snatched at the cigarettes in his case, ripping two of them in half against the elastic braid in his attempt to release one. He could easily have had Dakin marched back in front of him and made to face the consequences of his insubordination; but for good reason he chose to let the matter ride. Instead, he made his way along the corridor to the office of his lady superintendant of clerical staff, Cybil Kelsett. As he opened her door, she looked up from her work. It took only a nod from the colonel for her to know what was required.

~~~

As always, the colonel made contact in a busy, public place. He worked on the theory that should he ever be challenged, it would be far easier to devise a plausible story if he had been surrounded by people and everyday activity. Getting off the crowded omnibus at Victoria Embankment, he walked purposefully towards a bench a few yards away from the landmark of Cleopatra's Needle. There, he sat down and waited.

Right on time, Miss Kelsett appeared. The very business-like supervisor, dressed in a simple monochrome tunic and skirt, approached confidently and sat on the bench. Placing her bag over the envelope of Dakin's reports, located between her and the colonel, she enquired in her no-nonsense, well-educated voice, 'Destroy them or simply have them disappear, sir?'
~~~

The colonel remained expressionless, continuing only to stare forwards. Eventually, he glanced down at the envelope and gave his answer. 'Disappear for now.'

'It's over, isn't it?' stated the woman, with some disappointment in her voice.

'Probably once more,' the colonel answered honestly.

'I see. Oh well, all good things must come to an end I suppose.'

'Good' was very much an understatement, and really Miss Kelsett knew it, because she and the colonel had, for the last twelve months, been involved in an arrangement that had brought her more money than she could have ever have dreamed possible.

'And what of Mr Dakin?'

The colonel's eyes were cruel, although his tone was only one of indifference. 'Let's not worry about Mr Dakin, shall we?' He stood up and tipped his hat.

Later that evening, at the rear of a rundown terraced property, Dakin's cat was meowing endlessly by her owner's back door. The creature of habit knew that Dakin should have returned by now. The newspapers the following day showed why he hadn't. The headline merited only a single column:

BODY FOUND IN THAMES.

Chapter 18

She gasped in utter surprise. The last person Mrs Sowerby could have imagined seeing on opening the door was actually standing in front of her, sporting a large grin. But nobody was meant to know where she and Daniel were staying.

'Hello, Mrs Sowerby. Long time, no see!' said Wilson, producing a bigger smile.

The housekeeper looked dumbfounded. It took her a few moments to fully grasp the situation. After all, it had been well over a year since she'd last seen him. Eventually, she returned his smile. 'Peter! What a lovely surprise,' she said, using the name she knew him by. She would have given the world to reach out her hand, touch his face and kiss his cheek; but she simply couldn't. All she could manage was, 'I can't quite believe it. How are you? And how on earth did you know I was here?'

Wilson lifted his eyebrows and inclined his head mischievously. 'I could be tempted to tell everything for one of your delicious biscuits,' he joked.

Mrs Sowerby gave a little laugh, remembering how the

biscuit tin would always miraculously end up empty after his visits. 'You'd better come in. I have to tell you, though, Professor Sharpe won't be home until much later tonight.'

'It's not the professor I'm here to see, Mrs Sowerby … It's you!'

One might well wonder why Wilson was visiting Mrs Sowerby, and under a different name. It certainly wasn't to become re-acquainted with the housekeeper's biscuits. The answer to the conundrum was to be found back in Sheffield, eighteen months earlier.

~~~

The city library, where Judge Sanderson first took the technical drawings of military hardware, had not proved to be the best of venues for their assignations. Apart from the constant risk of being spotted and challenged, the area offered insufficient light to produce adequate photographs. A new place had to be found, but the judge was unwilling to keep lugging the drawings to different locations in the city. The proposal he came up with was to take the plans home with him. Then a photographer could visit, perhaps in the guise of a new gardener. The judge had been astute enough to realise that, if he were ever discovered, this solution would at least offer the plausible excuse that he needed to study the documents
~~~

for possible copyright infringement.

The photographer chosen for the task was one of Steinhauer's young and eager recruits with a flair for creative work. That person was Arthur Wilson.

Using the alias Peter Tyler, Wilson would turn up at the judge's house, usually on a weekly basis, and set up his equipment in the summerhouse. There, he was free to lay out any particularly large plan drawings and take aerial shots from a pair of step ladders. As far as Mrs Sowerby was concerned, he was simply photographing and documenting potted plants to help the judge with his passion for horticulture.

On 'Peter's' visits, she would invite the young man into the kitchen for coffee and be intrigued by his extensive knowledge of renaissance art. As the weeks passed, Wilson became a firm favourite with Mrs Sowerby, who soon began to look forward immensely to their chats. To her, he was a clever and talented individual who made her laugh. What added further to her admiration for him was seeing how well he interacted with Daniel. It seemed as if Wilson could instantly relate to the boy's significant difficulties and emotional vulnerability. He remembered, as a child, experiencing his own similar and unusual responses to situations.

Daniel took to the new visitor immediately. One day, he became particularly excited when told to bring his soldiers to the summerhouse. There, Wilson helped him prepare a battle scene on the floor, and then allowed him to view the image through the focusing hood of his camera. On the photographer's next visit, he gave Daniel a print of the photo. The boy looked at it and was truly mesmerised.

Mrs Sowerby just stood staring at Wilson. Had he looked at her more intently at that precise moment, he would have seen someone not just intrigued by him: he would have seen a woman truly infatuated.

At first Elsie Sowerby had had no more than the odd thought of Wilson, wondering what he might be doing at a particular moment. Her thoughts, however, quickly became all-absorbing. She had believed that the prospect of a man she could call her own had long since been extinguished; but Wilson, quite unintentionally, awakened her suppressed feelings. She needed to know all about him, wanted to be around him. Nevertheless, she always tried to counter her feelings with a dose of reality. She was ten years older than him. A relationship was not possible, she continually told herself.

Alone at night, she would slap her face, wanting to purge herself of any thoughts of him. But, when Wilson failed to visit for two weeks, she became distraught, and finally acknowledged to herself that she had fallen in love. The object of her love, though, had no idea of this, for Mrs Sowerby never gave Wilson any indication of how she felt towards him. Although all she wanted to do was reach out and touch his hand, her inhibitions would never allow it.

In the end, far from being blessed by cupid's golden dart, Elsie Sowerby was wounded by an arrow of lead when Wilson was moved to London at short notice.

~~~

As with any dampened desire, to rekindle it took only the slightest spark. On seeing Wilson once more, Mrs Sowerby was immediately consumed with longing. Nothing could have prepared her for how she was feeling. Her heart was racing in a way she had never imagined possible. He had lost none of his appeal.

'Why on earth would you want to see me?' she asked, not really caring what the answer might be. That he wanted to see her was all that mattered. His response took her by surprise.

'I don't have time to explain everything, but you have to trust me when I say that you and Daniel are in terrible danger.'

Mrs Sowerby stood looking totally confused.

'I need to get both of you somewhere safe, and quickly,' Wilson insisted.
~~~

'I'm sorry, Peter, but I don't understand.'

'Think back to the dinner party the other night.'

'Yes. What about it?'

'Did you recognise the man who was a guest?'

'What, Mr Green?'

'Yes.'

'No I can't say as I knew him.'

Their conversation was interrupted by Daniel, who appeared from the parlour. He looked towards Wilson without any expression on his face. Mrs Sowerby took hold of his hand.

'You remember Peter, don't you, Daniel? He was —'

Before she'd had time to finish, Daniel moved forward, without saying a word, and wrapped his arms around Wilson, resting his cheek against the man's chest.

It was heartwarming to see. Wilson responded by gently patting the boy's back and speaking softly. 'Hello, soldier. And how are you?'

But Wilson knew time was running out. He turned his attention back to Mrs Sowerby. 'You must pack some things and come with me, without delay.'

'But Peter, I can't just up and leave.'

'Please! Green will be here any moment and, believe me, his intentions are not good.'

'Who is he?'

'I believe he visited the judge once or twice, but I'm

sure he would have used another name.'

Wilson checked his pocket watch yet again. He ran his hand nervously over his face. 'Do you trust me, Mrs Sowerby?'

'Yes, of course, but —'

'Then please let me explain everything later. Meanwhile, you must go and pack a few things.'

The three of them managed to avoid Green by only minutes as they fled the Sharpes' home and headed for a run-down 'safe house' in the East End. There wasn't even time for Mrs Sowerby to leave Mary a message. 'Heaven knows what she'll think,' she kept protesting. But Wilson knew that should be the least of her worries.

Travelling across the city with just a small suitcase for her and Daniel, the housekeeper kept racking her brains, trying to remember if she'd met Green before. Closing her eyes, she thought back to the dinner party and tried to visualise him. All the time, she kept coming back to his eyes, recalling how dark and emotionless they had appeared. She tracked around the image she held of his face, willing herself to identify a feature she could place, but there was nothing.

Wilson really didn't care whether she remembered or not. All that mattered was that he'd saved the lives of two people he regarded with affection. He leant his head back against the carriage seat and relaxed. Had it not been for

Green ringing him earlier in the day, insisting they meet at the Sharpes' that afternoon, Mrs Sowerby and Daniel would almost certainly now be dead.

Peering out of the window, considering what excuse he would give Green for not showing up, Wilson caught the reflection of Mrs Sowerby looking at him intently. He turned to face her and watched as she produced a delicate smile. For the first time, he realised just how lovely a woman Elsie Sowerby was.

Chapter 19

Standing looking down the street towards the safe house, Mrs Sowerby could only draw a deep breath and sincerely hope that the interior was better than the exterior. To say that it was run down was being much too kind: the whole place was a slum. It was nothing she hadn't seen before. In fact, it wasn't far removed from what she'd grown up in. But over the years, she had raised herself beyond abject poverty and now had no desire to return to it.

Wilson could only apologise as they strode over the mounds of rubble and bits of broken furniture which children had made into play barricades. Daniel seemed unconcerned, even curious. Eventually, they reached a passageway which led to the rear of the terraced houses. Peering into the dreary, dank, moss-covered brick opening, Mrs Sowerby immediately remembered the cold winter nights of her childhood, when she'd had to walk through similar desperate snickets to get home, often encountering any number of unsavoury sights.

After turning the key, Wilson gave the door several good barges with his shoulder to free it and allow it to swing open. He held out his arm, inviting her in. With trepidation Mrs Sowerby entered. But given what Wilson had told her about Green's plans, she was just thankful that she and Daniel were out of harm's way. Besides which, she nurtured the hope that their stay would only be for a couple of days.

Once inside the house, Mrs Sowerby was surprised to find the interior was actually in very good decorative order. Not only that, but the place was immaculately clean and tidy and included some pieces of new-looking furniture. In one of the bedrooms, the mattress was still in its cloth wrapping.

'Well! … That will teach me not to judge a book by its cover,' she stated, in a tone of pleasant surprise.

'I thought you'd at least approve of this bit,' replied Wilson. He closed the door, giving a sigh of relief that they had all finally made it.

The two-up-two-down property, for which the artist had been given the responsibility of holding the keys, had only recently been acquired. The last tenant had been the flamboyant actor, Henry Shepherd, whose addiction to tidying and cleanliness had made a little haven in the midst of the squalor of Ivy Street.

Within the hour, fires had been lit and warmth began spreading through the cold, whitewashed rooms. Wilson knew he was taking a huge risk coming here, but he had no real alternative. Use of his own, rented, house would have been even more dangerous. He hoped that by tomorrow, he would have been able to find another place for Mrs Sowerby and Daniel to stay, preferably far away from London.

He sat in the armchair wondering how best to proceed. Would he be able to fool Green for long, if at all, he wondered. Only time would tell.

The door to the room opened, distracting his train of thought. Mrs Sowerby sank onto the sofa opposite his.

'Asleep?' enquired Wilson, referring to Daniel.

'Finally! I never thought he'd settle. It's been such a long, hectic day for him … for all of us.'

'You do accept I had to get you out, Mrs Sowerby?'

'Of course,' she said and paused briefly. With determination, she then carried on, 'Peter, perhaps you'd call me Elsie from now on. I know to you I'm old, but —'

'You're not old, Mrs Sow… sorry, Elsie.' He playfully scratched his chin whilst looking her up and down. Shrugging his shoulders, he suggested, 'Twenty-five.'

'Huh! I wish I were.'

'Twenty-six then, maximum.'

'No! … Peter, I'm thirty-three.'

'Oh dear. Well, I guess we'd better get you booked in for a plot sooner rather than later.'

He laughed whilst trying to dodge the cushion she

flung at him.

Sitting opposite each other in the tiny front room, the pair were finally able to talk at length. Mrs Sowerby wanted so much to try and hint at her feelings for him, but first she had to reveal the lie of her marriage. In the end, the truth simply found its way out.

'… but you see, Peter, there is no Mr Sowerby.' She fanned out her hands in front of her face trying to maintain her composure and hold back the tears. Overcome partly by embarrassment, partly by guilt, she cast her head downwards. 'There never was.' Clutching a small handkerchief tightly in her hands, the tears finally came. She bounced her hands up and down on her knees, angry that she couldn't control her emotions. 'And now I'm crying and look such a fool.'

'No, no. You're not a fool. You simply did what you felt was right for you at the time.' Wilson's voice was soft and reassuring.

'But I lied, Peter, and I don't like lying.' She thought back to the day she had told Judge Sanderson she was married. 'But once you've told people, that's it: there's no going back.'

Wilson didn't need reminding of that fact. And, in his case, not only was there no going back, there was no going forward either, not whilst there was the constant threat of Green discovering what he was up to. How would he ever be able to explain to the woman gazing longingly at him the depth of his deceit? How would she react, should she ever know that his life was just one lie after another?

Even what he'd told her so far wasn't the whole truth. Perhaps, he hoped, she could be kept under the illusion that, through Green's past acquaintance with the judge, she and Daniel had simply shown up in the wrong place at the wrong time. Did she really have to know that he was as deeply involved as Green?

She continued to stare at him, her cheeks wet with tears. Wilson suddenly had the urge to reach out and wipe them away. His stomach began to churn nervously.

Moving to sit beside her on the sofa, he covered her hands with his. 'It's all right, I understand. Really I do.'

Taking the handkerchief from her hand, he started to gently wipe away her tears. She felt herself flush and begin to tremble, overwhelmed by an aching need for him not to stop. Soon, desire for him had pushed every other emotion into the background. Never before had she experienced feelings so strong. Nevertheless, her natural reactions took over, and she felt herself stiffen like a board. 'For god's sake, woman, will you just relax,' an inner voice objected. 'All he's done is hold your damned hand!'

Slowly he moved his lips towards her cheek, and then kissed it.

'Oh, dear lord above! Now you can panic,' the inner voice agreed.

As the next morning dawned, her whole body was still suffused with an exquisite excitement. Stretching out and touching him, as he lay naked beside her, she wondered how she had ever managed to go this long without feeling the joy of a man's love.

~~~

Wilson had an uneasy sensation in his gut. It was the same every time Green came to see him. He tapped his pencil across his palm anxiously, rehearsing his story once more. Glancing over to the clock, he was surprised that Green hadn't been up to the studio yet. Second guessing what might have delayed his colleague only unnerved him even more.

Just when he thought Green wasn't going to arrive, the door to the studio swung open and the man swaggered in, wasting no time in unleashing his caustic tongue. 'And here I was thinking you must have been hit by a bus or met with an end equally as pleasing.'

Wilson ignored the comment and waited.

'So?'

'If you're referring to me not meeting you yesterday, I'm sorry.'
~~~

Green gave a grimace. 'A golden opportunity wasted.'

'The tube got diverted at Moorgate. Then it was held up at Angel. By the time I got back to Kings Cross, I assumed you'd have gone, so I didn't carry on. Sorry. There was no way of letting you know.'

The excuse was a simple one; in fact, so simple, it sounded pathetic. But Wilson's alibi was completely watertight, because that was exactly what had happened to the 4.15 tube train to Finsbury Park. The only difference was that the artist had not been on it. He'd boarded the one that came along ten minutes later. But he knew Green wouldn't be able to prove anything one way or the other. Wilson realised, though, that he now needed to play the game, and he glanced around furtively, before leaning forward and quietly asking, 'I take it everything went to plan?'

An angry look spread across Green's face. Through gritted teeth he gave his reply, 'No, it bloody well did not go to plan.' Then, with ease, he reverted to a calm exterior and concluded without any hesitation, 'But next time it will.'

Wilson vowed to himself there wouldn't be a next time, but he needed a couple of days to find his new lover and Daniel a safe alternative place to stay. His mind drifted back to the previous evening. What he would give to be kissing her again. When they'd known each other previously, he'd had only a vague, friendly interest in Elsie Sowerby. Now, he couldn't get her out of his mind. Like a smitten schoolboy, his every thought was of her.

'I received a message from Steinhauer this morning,' announced Green.

Not really interested, Wilson gave a nonchalant response. 'Oh?'

'Yes, apparently there's a Swedish agent due through Tilbury later today. We need to house him for several days before he travels up north. I need the keys for Ivy Street.'

Wilson immediately went pale, his stomach feeling the sudden charge of fear. He didn't answer. All his tender images began crashing down before him. What could he do? He stood there in panic.

'Did you hear me? I said, I need the keys for —'

'Yes, I heard,' Wilson interrupted, trying to appear attentive. 'It's just … er … I'm not too sure where I've put them,' he muttered.

'Well, you'd better bloody well find them, and quickly,' retorted Green, already beginning to wonder what his fellow agent might be up to.

'I'm sure they're somewhere safe. Perhaps I could meet you with them later on?'

Wilson couldn't have appeared more unconvincing, whilst Green couldn't have been more adept at sensing something was wrong. There was nobody better at detecting when a man was lying. But why should he need to lie, wondered Green. Recalling their recent conversation, he was soon pondering: what if Wilson hadn't been delayed on that tube? What if he had arrived just before he did? And, what if he had been intent on rescuing Mrs Sowerby and the boy all along? After all, the artist had expressed an inexplicable curiosity and sympathy for the pair. Moments later, Green had put two and two together and come up with the possibility that Wilson might actually be hiding the two people he so desperately needed to find.

Changing his expression, as if by flicking a switch, Green gave a grin. 'Yes, I'm sure you've put the keys somewhere safe.' With a glance at the clock, he finished the conversation, 'I'll meet you at seven o'clock outside Old Street Station.'

Both men knew that they had to act quickly. Each needed to prepare a plan. By mid-afternoon, each had finalized his tactics.

Mrs Sowerby began to open the door cautiously. A myriad of doubts was going through her mind. Would he still be as excited as she was? Would he still feel the same as he had the night before? But suddenly another thought crossed her mind. What if —?

'Hello …,' the voice started.

Chapter 20

Arriving back home from visiting Elliott in hospital, Mary and Ann thought it seemed very strange that, at nearly seven o'clock in the evening, Mrs Sowerby and Daniel weren't in the house. In fact, Mary couldn't even recall her housekeeper saying she was going out. But, with all her attention focused on the Elliott's crisis, it wouldn't have surprised her if she had been told and just clean forgotten. She looked around for any sign of a note, but there was nothing. Her concern increased when Ann confirmed that Mrs Sowerby had mentioned preparing dinner for seven thirty. Her thoughts turned to whether her housekeeper had gone out to get something and met with an accident.

A phone call to the local police station confirmed that no accidents had been reported in the vicinity.

By eight o'clock Mary had started to contact each district police station in turn, but every time the answer was the same – no incidents reported involving people by the name of Elsie Sowerby or Daniel Sanderson.

It all remained very confusing. Mary and Ann started exploring other possibilities. Perhaps, for some reason,

Mrs Sowerby had decided to return to Sheffield. Maybe she had received some bad news about her family and had to leave suddenly. The possibilities were endless, but the women always came back to the same point: Mrs Sowerby was far too conscientious to disappear without leaving a note. As much as they hated even contemplating it, they were soon considering the prospect of a far more sinister occurrence.

When Tom arrived home at after ten o'clock, his wife and Ann were convinced something terrible had happened. It took a while for him to persuade them that there would be a logical explanation. He picked up the phone to try the one thing he might be able to influence – ringing each emergency hospital and checking their records of new admissions.

Greeted by the same operator who had already patched through the last twenty calls that Mary had made, Tom was surprised at her instinctive reaction. 'I'm not altogether sure there are any more police stations, Mrs Sharpe.'

'Sorry?' said Tom, pulling the earpiece away from his ear and looking confused.

It took some explaining from Mary for it all to make sense. Tom continued with his calls, but all of them were to no avail. In the end, it was agreed to wait another hour and then, if there was no sign of them, Tom would report Mrs Sowerby and Daniel as missing.

The following morning at the breakfast table was a somewhat quiet affair, with each person picking up their thoughts from the previous evening and re-analysing the situation. Tom checked his watch and decided he must make a move; otherwise he'd miss the tube. He leant over the table to kiss Mary. 'Let's hope the police come up with something, eh.' Grabbing his bag, he was suddenly gone.

'Mmm …' mused Mary.

'They must come up with something surely. People don't just disappear without trace,' commented Ann.

But Mary knew only too well from the experience she'd had with her brother, Walter, that disappearing without trace wasn't difficult.

Nothing did come from the police, although it eventually appeared their help would not be needed. Before dinner that evening, Mary answered a knock on the door. Standing on the step, a young boy called out, 'Telegram for Mrs Sharpe, miss.'

'Yes, that's me,' replied Mary, taking the piece of paper from him.

She gave the boy tuppence for his trouble, closed the door and read the brief message:

REALLY SORRY TO LEAVE AT SUCH SHORT NOTICE. BROTHER TAKEN SERIOUSLY ILL IN BRIGHTON. WILL CALL YOU ASAP.
E. SOWERBY

'Well at least we know she's safe,' said Mary and handed the telegram over to Ann to read.

Ann thought about the situation for a moment. 'But why did she have to take Daniel? She could have waited until we got home and then gone.'

'Perhaps she just wanted to catch a train as soon as she could.'

'Mmm. I know it sounds awful, Mary, but it still appears a bit suspicious to me.'

Ann was right to be apprehensive, for the telegram hadn't come from Mrs Sowerby at all.

~~~

By the end of his meeting with Wilson, Green didn't believe a word about the keys, and he sensed that Mrs Sowerby and Daniel were being sheltered in the safe house. Wilson knew he had almost certainly been found out and had to find a way to get to Ivy Street first. Acting quickly became imperative, and the one thing that should have bought Wilson time over his colleague was knowing that Green had to be back in the operating theatre for another hour that afternoon.

However, relying on his knowledge of Green's schedule was Wilson's undoing.

On leaving the hospital, as always, the artist opted for
~~~

a short cut at the rear of the building by taking the outside fire escape down onto the yard below. After passing three large archways where coal was stored, it was possible to get onto the main road, saving time. In one of the arches Green lurked, hidden from view, and impatiently tapping the end of a rounded wooden club across the palm of his hand. Time was the thing that he too didn't have.

At last, he heard Wilson approaching.

'Psst!' called a voice out of the darkness, causing Wilson to pull up. After a moment's hesitation, he walked into the archway, curious to see who was there. Unable to see anyone he started to back out, then felt the full force of the club against the back of his head. He fell forwards onto the ground like a felled tree. Green rolled him over with his foot. Although he knew just where to strike the head and exactly how much pressure to use, he still felt for a pulse and then gave a wry smile. Just as planned, Wilson was out cold but still alive. All that Green needed to do now was to inject his victim with enough sedative to last several hours and to leave him hidden until he got back from Ivy Street.

In the safe house, Mrs Sowerby sat on the sofa fumbling desperately with her hands, horrified by the commotion coming from upstairs. Eventually, the shouting, banging and thumps moved from the bedroom to the stairs. She held her hands over her ears wanting it all just to stop.

At last it did. The door flew open and Green dragged the protesting Daniel into the room. He threw him down on the sofa next to his nurse.

The distraught boy started to tap his head and rock. Mrs Sowerby tried desperately to calm him.

'Why don't you just finish what you came here to do,' she snapped at Green.

Green pierced her with his cruel, soulless eyes, but didn't say anything.

To kill them had certainly been his intention until yesterday; but then he had been told the arrangement he was party to would happen only once more. That news had changed everything. He would still carry out his intentions towards the woman and the boy; and, likewise, he would still murder Wilson; but for the moment he needed them alive. His plan needed a phone call from Mrs Sowerby to Mary. This was the only sure way of getting Mary to board the train. With regards to Wilson, he was the only one able to draw that last code.

As with all complex plans, in order for this one to work effectively, everything had to come together at just the right time. The only problem for Green was that he didn't yet have an exact date for when things would happen. Until then, he had to make sure that Wilson was kept apart from Mrs Sowerby and Daniel. To achieve this, he decided to keep the housekeeper and the boy locked up in a room in his special warehouse. This was a location guaranteed to inflict misery and foreboding.

Chapter 21

Returning to the hospital from Ivy Street, Green peered out of the window and raised the alarm about seeing someone lying unconscious in the coal stores. He then watched from a distance as orderlies brought Wilson into the emergency room for treatment and doctors began assessing him.

The smell of ammonium carbonate and perfume rising up through his nostrils made Wilson stir, then pull away. After a while he was fully conscious again, but the duty doctor didn't get a chance to ask any questions before his patient was insisting on knowing the time.

'Just gone half past eight at night,' confirmed the doctor.

'Damn!'

Cautiously feeling the massive lump that stood out prominently on the back of his head, Wilson slowly began to recall things and realised that he had been attacked, although he couldn't remember seeing the person who had struck him. He began to curse.

'Just lie back, sir. We'll —'

'No!' interrupted Wilson, firmly. 'I'm fine. I've got to go.'

'Sir, you could be badly concussed.'

Trying to get off the bed and to his feet, Wilson was pulled back by the doctor.

'I'm alright, damn you.'

A war of words broke out until Green came over and intervened. With a staged expression of surprise, he cried, 'Arthur! Whatever has happened to you?'

By this point, there were half a dozen people grouped around Wilson. This, and the throbbing in his head made any effort at thinking straight almost impossible. Eventually, he snapped. 'For God's sake, just leave me alone!'

Green agreed with the others present that he would take over from here and, when everyone had left and calm had been restored, he checked Wilson's head, whilst listening to the man explaining what had happened.

'Nathan, can you give something for the pain?'

'Of course,' replied Green, now convinced that Wilson had no idea who had knocked him unconscious. 'I'll arrange for a nurse to bring you something. Meanwhile, you should stay in overnight and I'll look in on you tomorrow.'

Giving his sickly smile, Green turned to leave, content that his objective had been successfully achieved.

Wilson, however, had no intention of staying. All he wanted to do was to get to Ivy Street. Within half an hour he was walking towards the tube station, all the while scratching the itching in the fold of his arm.

A lack of any light, sound or greeting as he opened the door immediately indicated to him there was something wrong. Wandering around the house, calling out their names, merely confirmed that Elsie Sowerby and Daniel had gone. Wilson sank into the sofa in desperation. There could only be three possibilities, he thought. Either Elsie had had a change of heart and just decided to go; or the pair had been discovered and fled; or, and most likely, Green had beaten him to the house and taken them away against their will.

The itching on his arm was now driving Wilson crazy. In frustration he ripped off his jacket and pulled up his sleeve to reveal a sore red ring on his skin. He pulled his eyebrows together, trying to remember when he'd had this sensation before. Eventually, he saw the small pin prick over his vein and realised it was an allergic reaction to an injection, just like the last time he had had an anesthetic. Slowly it began to dawn on him who might be responsible. 'Of course,' he cried, recalling entering the coal store and smelling disinfectant. He remembered that, just hours before, Green had spilt half a bottle on his trousers.

'The bastard!' he screamed. 'So it was him that attacked me and then plunged god knows what into my vein. Bastard! Bastard!' he repeatedly spat, punching the cushion beside him. The trouble was that he knew he couldn't prove any of it. All the same, he now would have no qualms in killing Green. 'An eye for an eye,' he cried, convinced his fellow agent would already have taken the lives of Mrs Sowerby and Daniel.

Wilson's anger soon turned to a feeling of utter helplessness. He pulled his hands over his face, fighting back his tears. On lifting his head, he saw Elsie's shawl behind a cushion. Holding it against his cheek, he remembered how he'd taken it off her shoulders. How nervous she had been at the first, tender touch of a man. He pictured her sweet face lying beside his, contented and free from inhibition. The more he tried to forget things, the more the memory lingered. And what of Daniel? After all the boy had already endured, now this.

A distraught Wilson threw down the shawl as the anger welled up in him once more. 'Bastard!' he again cried. Finally, he stood up with determination. He wouldn't wait any longer; he had to have retribution.

The door to the safe-house slammed shut. Another brief chapter in the history of Ivy Street was over.

~~~

In the quiet of night, every noise in the hospital corridor, despite its linoleum floor, seemed to carry far into the distance. And when Wilson's footsteps were heard
~~~

approaching, almost marching in quick time, the heads of inquisitive nursing staff naturally turned. Amongst them was Green, working his final hour of a long shift.

He pulled back slightly, allowing the pillar to obscure him, and watched as Wilson strode past, with an intent in his eyes the like of which Green had never before witnessed in the artist.

'Where's Dr Green?' he heard Wilson shout at a young nurse.

The girl flinched at his tone. 'Er … He was here,' she said, looking around.

Green leant back further behind the pillar.

'He might have gone to the ward on B floor,' suggested the nurse, not really having a clue but just wanting to get away from Wilson. The look of hatred in his eyes frightened her.

Green assumed Wilson had been to Ivy Street or somehow found out the truth. He pondered his options. Either he could leave quickly; or he could go back to his office to get his revolver and deal with the situation decisively. The doctor knew it had to be the latter.

Luckily for Green, he knew all the different back stairways between floors, and a quick shortcut that would take him to near his office was tucked away behind him, towards the linen store. He leapt up the tiny winding stairs and peeped through the glass window in the door.

After catching his breath for a moment, he cautiously edged out of the stairway and made his way to his office. Once inside, he ripped open his desk drawer and dropped a false back to reveal a pistol with silencer. Wiping the sweat away from his brow, Green cocked the gun. The familiar sound always made him feel in control.

'I think he may be in his office,' Green heard a voice saying from the corridor. Quickly, he rushed to switch off the light and hid behind the door. He only just made it before the handle turned and Wilson entered the room. The light from the corridor shone straight ahead, but not enough for him to see properly.

A thoroughly agitated Wilson stepped forward, holding a knife in his hand like a dagger. Suddenly the room was plunged into darkness as the door slammed shut behind him. He spun round in panic.

Green flicked the light switch. 'Hello Arthur! Did you want me for anything in particular?' he said sarcastically, pointing his gun towards Wilson's head. Calmly he gestured at the knife. 'Not much use against a gun is it? Put it on the desk.'

'You evil bastard,' snarled Wilson.

'So, I'm told!'

Wilson took a step forward ready to lunge with the knife, but pulled back as Green flexed his arm and then held the pistol nearer to his head.

'Put it on the desk,' reaffirmed Green, this time with menace.

'Go ahead! Shoot me, just like you did Elsie and Daniel no doubt.'

It took a split second for it to register. Green gave a snigger. 'Elsie? Not Mrs Sowerby? So that's it. You've fallen for the delightful housekeeper. Well, bless.'

Wilson finally threw the knife onto the desk in defeat. 'Just tell me where you've put the bodies.'

'Bodies! You've got things all wrong, Arthur. Your precious Elsie and the boy aren't dead. They're just somewhere safe, that's all. Somewhere where I can keep an eye on them.'

Hearing those words seemed to lift the whole weight of sadness off Wilson's shoulders. He took a deep breath, barely able to disguise his elation. Equally, he was confused. 'But I thought you wanted …' The artist paused, not wanting to use the words, but really there wasn't an alternative, '… to kill them.'

'Things have changed.'

'I want to see them,' demanded Wilson.

'First, you help me … You paint one last code.'

Wilson once more gave a frown of confusion. 'Last code?'

'Yes. The project is being ended. There'll be just one more.'

'And if I don't do it?'

Green smiled smugly. 'I think holding your lover and

the boy is my surety that you will.'

Nibbling at his lip nervously, Wilson contemplated the situation. In the end, he knew that to stand any chance of seeing Elsie and Daniel again, he'd have to concede. 'All right. I'll do the code if we agree a mutual swap, and on my terms. I need to ensure we can just disappear quietly.'

Green considered the proposal, for the benefit of the whole charade, but he knew exactly how he would handle things from here. For now, though, he would give Wilson his assurance. 'Very good. I'll talk with Steinhauer and be in touch.'

'First, prove to me they're alive,' said Wilson, stipulating his first demand.

Green thought for a second. 'As you wish. Tomorrow, I'll arrange for her to telephone you here at work around two o'clock.'

~~~

Sitting in his study gazing at Mary's picture, Green sighed and massaged the back of his neck, trying to loosen his tense muscles. Had he made the right decision, he wondered. Once more, he looked down at Mary's face and lightly ran his finger across her lips. As always, it didn't take much for Green to enter his world of fantasy. Curiously though, in imagining himself with Mary, he
~~~

never went beyond a tender touch. Whilst he would visualise and stroke her body, never once did he imagine them making love.

His concentration was broken by the mantle clock chiming the hour. Green leant over and reached for his bag. From inside he pulled out a syringe and flicked at the needle. The colourless solution gently trickled over the tip.

It was time.

From outside his sister's room, he slowly opened the door and entered. Maude was sitting at her dressing table, her fingers gently feeling at the large scar that tracked from her damaged nose, down across her cheek until finally it disappeared under what was left of her ear.

Maude looked up at her brother. Always in discomfort, she attempted a smile.

'When Nathan? When will you be able to do it?' she pleaded, not sure how many more injections of morphine she could endure. For some time after the operation had taken place, there had been no problems; but recently her facial tissue had started to spasm and cause her terrible pain.

Reluctantly, she laid out her arm for her brother to administer the drug. Afterwards he knelt down beside her and held his sister in a tight embrace. For a while they remained holding each other until, eventually, he kissed her head and slowly pulled away. Lifting up her chin, he smiled. 'Any day now. I've found a suitable clinic near Peterborough. We'll need to arrange for you to stay somewhere nearby.'

He watched Maude's face light up with joy. Little did she realise that this surgery would almost certainly mean her death. It beggared belief that Green was prepared to carry out an operation to reconstruct his sister's face using another person's transplanted tissue and skin. But then Green had always been deluded enough to think that his skill with a scalpel could ultimately defy the rules of biology and organ rejection. He showed no real concern that any transplant surgery performed thus far had always spectacularly failed. All that concerned him was that he shouldn't come home one day to find his sister had taken her life because he wouldn't treat her.

'The woman whose face ... Will she be beautiful?' Maude innocently asked.

Of that he could definitely assure her.

It had been Green's worst ever dilemma. Given more time, he would have simply found someone else as a suitable donor; but time was fast running out. He had had to make a decision. Given the similarity between the two women's facial features, Green had agonised over what to do. In the end, it came down to blood being thicker than water. His mind was suddenly clear; he had to entice Mary to Peterborough, where he would sacrifice her life in order to save his sister's. For Maude, he was prepared to try anything.

Chapter 22

Despite not wanting to leave London and return to Sheffield, Ann felt she had little choice. Elliott would be hospitalized for at least another week, and she had to return to their boys, who were due back at school on the following Monday.

Having visited her husband for the last time, she met with Tom in his office to say a final farewell.

They sat and chatted for a while, until interrupted by a tap on the door

'Enter!' Tom boomed playfully.

Sister Lucas walked in holding a couple of patient files, although she stopped immediately on seeing Ann sitting on the chair opposite Tom's desk. 'Oh, I'm terribly sorry, professor, I didn't realise you had a patient.'

Tom was in an especially mischievous mood. 'No, no. This isn't a patient, sister. This lady here is my mistress.'

Even knowing his devilish sense of humour, Ann was slightly shocked at Tom's comment. To the sister though, it was typical of their daily banter. 'Another one, Professor Sharpe,' she said. 'This is becoming quite a habit.' Then, turning to address Ann, she gave a smile. 'Good morning, Madam.'

Ann, who by now was totally bewildered by the bizarre conversation, hesitantly replied, 'Er …yes, good morning to you.'

She thought Tom would at least explain who she really was. But he never did. Instead, he looked towards the files in the sister's hand and asked, 'Anything quick?'

'Well, yes, if you don't mind. Could I just check with you the medication for these two patients,' replied the sister, handing over the files.

Tom flicked through the pages of the first one, checking his notes. He began muttering, '… Chloral hydrate … three times every four hours.' Pausing, he looked up at the sister, wanting a clue.

'You haven't stated a measure, professor,' the sister enlightened him.

'Of course!' Tom slapped his forehead. 'Sorry. Seven grains,' he confirmed and wrote it on the sheet.

Proceeding to open the second file, he gave a grin. 'Ah, Mr Elliott. What have I managed to miss here?'

'Perhaps something to stop him talking so much,' joked the sister. 'The man has quite an opinion on … well, just about everything, Mr Sharpe. Including how I should be running my ward!'

'I see,' said Tom before turning towards Ann. 'What

do you reckon for your husband, Mrs Elliott? Arsenic? Or shall we have something less agonising?'

The sister, realising her blunder, placed her hand over her open mouth and looked sheepishly at Ann. All she could do was offer her apology. But Ann could quite appreciate what Sister Lucas was having to endure with Elliott as a patient.

'Don't worry,' she said and held up a finger to give her some friendly advice. 'The trick to managing my husband's opinions, sister, is to make him think that they're all his own.'

The room rang out with laughter.

~~~

Well, why don't you just —' suggested Elliott, before being cut short by the thoroughly frustrated Sister Lucas.

'Because, Mr Elliott, that is how we do it, how we've always done it, and whether you like it or not, that is how it's going to stay,' she said firmly.

'Fair enough,' replied Elliott, snapping his newspaper back in front of his face. 'In future I shall keep my opinions to myself.'

Oh, if only that could be the case, thought Sister Lucas as she placed the clipboard back at the end of Elliott's bed. Checking the traction on his leg, she decided to have the
~~~

last laugh, 'And no running off now, do you hear?'

From behind his newspaper, Elliott gave a silent and animated mock laugh. He allowed his head to fall back onto the pillow. It was going to be another long day, especially now Ann wouldn't be visiting him. Picking up his paper again, he flicked his eyes across the columns of print. A headline finally caught his attention: 'Crashed Zeppelin May Reveal German Secrets.' After reading the article, Elliott started to think again about Tom's theory on Daniel's reaction to the face drawings.

Calling over a nurse, he asked her to get his jacket and then fumbled through his pockets until he found Tom's piece of paper. He began to study the lines and systematically analyse the sequences of letters and numbers using his friend's theory. If nothing else, this was going to keep Elliott entertained for a while.

It also kept the other patients thoroughly amused, as they watched the engrossed probation officer nodding his head like a dog. First, looking up to follow a line, then down, right, up again, across left and finally down once more. After a while, he got into the rhythm and started to spell out words using each line length and direction to indicate a letter, just as Tom had suggested was the case.

Eventually Elliott was bobbing up and down and criss-crossing his head so much, he caught the attention of the duty nurse at the end of the ward. She walked over in concern and asked, 'Is everything all right, Mr Elliott?'

Of course he couldn't resist coding his answer as well as speaking it. 'Y E S   I' M   F I N E.'

'I'll fetch the sister,' cried the alarmed nurse.

When the sister arrived, Elliott was still moving his head about and spelling out his words. She sighed. 'What are we going to do with you, Mr Elliott?'

Elliott was suddenly in devilish mood. 'As a detainee once said to me, sister, "Send me somewhere out of the country, to sea for choice. I should be out of temptation on a sailing ship. Or an Indian wigwam village might do. Perhaps even a Bedouin encampment."'

His reply had the sister reaching out for the clipboard once more to verify that his medication really was correct.

Any further confrontation was avoided by Tom arriving on the ward to check on his friend's progress. Coming up alongside the bed, he asked, 'I trust you're behaving yourself, Robert?'

'Of course!'

Sister Lucas just opened her eyes wide.

After some deliberation, Tom agreed that, providing the x-rays showed no further complications, Elliott could be taken off traction the following day. 'At least then we can occasionally get you into a wheelchair or better still, on crutches.'

Needless to say, the sister's eyes opened even wider.

Seeing his piece of paper in Elliott's hand, Tom soon joined his friend in discussing the codes and what they could mean, although he could ill afford the time from his daily round. Eventually, he had to break away and return to the operating theatre, but he left Elliott with another interesting observation.

If they were interpreting the cipher correctly, then every group of lines began with the letter W followed, usually, by three other letters and at least three numbers. It was a start; but Elliott knew it meant nothing really. Was it a serial number? A product code? A result? A formula? If the War Office code breakers were having no success, then what chance did he have, he wondered.

By mid afternoon, Elliott's interest was waning. This, along with another strong dose of painkillers, saw him intermittently closing his eyes. Soon, he was fast asleep and snoring loudly. He was woken to be taken to x-ray, but after his next dose of medication, he slept solidly until the next morning.

On waking, he discovered to his joy that his leg was now out of traction and the space beside his bed was occupied by a wheelchair. He gave a grin and turned to the man in the next bed. 'They've only gone and —' He paused, seeing the next bed was now empty. In fact, it had been totally stripped down to the frame. Elliott looked over to his left.

'Died,' clarified the multiple amputee soldier. 'Lucky bastard!'

The futility of it all suddenly overwhelmed Elliott, as if he were a mere rock caught in a sand storm. He was completely used to seeing death; but as the orderlies brought in a new mattress, it brought home to him how normal – casual even – dying had become. The man in the neigbouring bed had been just eighteen years old.

For the rest of the morning Elliott felt quite sad. In a strange way, he felt guilty that he had been fast asleep when the soldier had passed away. By lunch time though, he'd managed to shake his blue mood, and he set about trying to maneuver himself from bed to wheelchair. After numerous comical failed attempts, he finally managed to make it and ended up sitting, exhausted, but proud, with his plastered leg resting on a splint-board and pointing straight ahead. Getting back, however, might prove to be less easy.

Glancing over to the empty bed, Elliott wondered who would be arriving next and when. It was only then that he noticed something. Had the mattress been made up, he would never have seen the label stitched on the top left corner. Printed on it were letters and numbers. Closer inspection showed them to be a stock number: WDK8293. He wheeled himself round to the side of his own mattress and eagerly pulled back the sheet corners.

Again the label had a similar number: WNP5346. More checks on other mattresses all revealed that the stock code always began with the letter W.

Had Elliott inadvertently stumbled on exactly what the code might relate to?

Full of excitement, he wanted to share his findings with Tom without delay. Being confined to a wheelchair with a plastered leg sticking out, however, was not conducive to traveling around the hospital looking for him. At least, not without some help. Mr Barber, further down the ward, seemed his best option.

'So how bored is bored, Mr Barber?' asked Elliott, with a mischievous glint in his eye.

'Very!' cried Mr Barber.

'Enough for a touch of adventure perhaps?'

Mr Barber seemed to be getting the picture. 'And would this adventure include a couple of patients and a wheelchair by chance?'

Elliott smiled. 'Possibly!'

When the sister was called to the ward, she was furious to find that two of her patients had suddenly disappeared. And knowing Elliott was friendly with Professor Sharpe, she had a good idea where they might be heading. Her hunch proved right, but she was too late to stop her two escapees entering the operating theatre department.

Nobody was more shocked than Tom to see a plastered

leg entering through the door of the annex to operating theatre 3, followed shortly after by its owner, crying out, 'Ah, there you are!'

'Robert! What on earth? … You can't just barge into a theatre area.'

'Yes, yes,' Elliott said, waving his hand as if it was a mere triviality. 'I've found what it means. The code!'

Tom remained flabbergast.

'The letters and numbers all relate to mattresses, Tom.'

Still unable to fully believe that Elliott had entered the restricted area, Tom ushered him back and helped wheel him to the department entrance and on towards the corridor. All the while, he berated his friend for what he'd done. But his exasperated words went in one ear and out of the other, as Elliott continued to explain his findings.

Finally, they pulled up.

'Robert, I don't want to hear any more about it right now,' Tom snapped. 'I'll come and see you later.' With that he turned to leave, shouting over his shoulder, 'And please go straight back to the ward.'

Elliott looked up at Mr Barber, who had hobbled his way through the whole affair. 'If there's one thing I've leant in life, it's that some people are never grateful.'

Sister Lucas suddenly turned the corner and proceeded straight towards them with a face like thunder. Each man braced himself.

'Ah, sister, I was just …' started Elliott, wanting to get in first.

If he hadn't already thoroughly blotted his copybook, he certainly had now.

~~~

By the time Tom got round to visiting Elliott, he had calmed down and could just about see the funnier side of events, even if at the time it hadn't been amusing. Despite his own often mischievous behaviour, the one thing about Tom which had to be admired was that he always took theatre procedures seriously. After all, he had helped to write many of them. On sitting down with Elliott, he quickly got his point over. 'All joking aside, Robert, you have to understand the massive risk posed by people, especially patients with possible infections, wandering around in clinical areas.'

Feeling duly reprimanded, Elliott offered to embark on a major charm offensive with Sister Lucas, although, in the end, it was agreed that it might be better for Tom to smooth the waters in his own way. Meanwhile, Elliott promised to try and be the model patient. How long that would last remained to be seen.

Both men sat discussing the exciting discovery about the code for quite some time. At last, Tom felt there was enough new information to take to Dakin
~~~

and his department code breakers. Little did he know that there was no longer a Mr Dakin in existence with whom to discuss matters further. It would take another coincidence before things could develop to a conclusion, and that coincidence was not long in coming.

The following day found Elliott keeping a low profile with the sister. He wheeled himself round to sit and talk with the quiet young soldier who was missing an arm and a leg, and had had a skin graft on his face. The man was busily painting on a small watercolour pad laid down on a lap table in front of him.

'That's really good,' said Elliott, before holding out his hand, 'We haven't properly introduced ourselves … Robert Elliott.'

The soldier released his brush, wanting to shake hands, but Elliott had held out his right hand. Quickly he realised it needed to be his left, and changed over.

'David Ashton,' said the man, finally able to give a firm handshake.

The pair talked for a good while, although Elliott had immediately recognised the fragility of the young man's state of mind. He didn't ask, but surmised that the scarred slash marks on the man's neck were the result of trying to end his life.

'Three times,' the soldier said, knowing Elliott was looking at his neck. Most visitors did. 'I haven't had the balls to take the blade right through yet … but one day I will!'

It pained Elliott to see anybody contemplating such an action. Throughout his career, he had always been able to see a brighter future for the disadvantaged. However, looking at the broken soldier in front of him, he began to question his own eternal optimism. Where would a ray of sunshine come from for this lad?

Elliott gave a genuine smile. He held his hand over that of the soldier. 'Never lose hope, young man.'

Perhaps hope was through his painting, thought Elliott and admired the vista of an imaginary grass meadow the soldier was painting. 'I wish I could draw.'

'Everyone says that. It's not hard. It's just practice really,' replied the soldier, rationally.

Elliott sighed. 'Huh, not in my case.'

'I can show you if you like.'

Seeing the soldier's enthusiasm made Elliott realise that this was where the man's sunshine would come from. 'Yes! I would like that. Thank you.'

Within half an hour, the probation officer had become the art student, listening to the theory of perspective, underpainting, dark over light and vice versa. At first, he had no real interest, but soon he found himself becoming absorbed in the subject and starting to ask more and more questions. Half an hour became an hour, which in turn became two hours, then nearly three. Once Elliott had picked up a brush and created his first wash effect, there was no stopping him. He was totally immersed in a whole new world.

Studying the soldier's painting once more, Elliott had a question. 'Why don't you just rub out all the pencil underneath?'

'Because it adds texture, makes everything look less rigid.'

Elliott scrunched up his nose. He didn't quite understand.

'Here, I'll show you,' said the soldier and, taking a pencil, he proceeded to sketch out tufts of grass in a line. Then, using his paintbrush, he lightly applied some colour. 'Right. Can you see how the pencil marks add elements of interesting shade?'

Elliott nodded.

'We'll let it dry and then rub them out.' After a couple of minutes, the soldier picked up his putty rubber and erased the pencil. 'There, see the difference?'

With his eyes beginning to open wide and a large grin rapidly spreading across his face, Elliott punched the air euphorically. He immediately knew this was how the code was being incorporated into the pictures. It was simple, yet perfectly brilliant. All Wilson had been doing was painting the mattress stock number in his picture of a face then skillfully disguising it by adding pencil strokes. Only when these were erased would the code become clearly visible.

'You, my friend, might just have become a hero!' cried Elliott.

Chapter 23

Speaking with Dakin's senior secretary, Emily Dewhirst, and learning of her boss's demise through drowning, left Tom shocked and feeling that all the wind had suddenly been taken out of his sails. Moments earlier he had been standing, with boyish anticipation, ready to reveal to Dakin the code discoveries he and Elliott had made. Now, with the man dead, he felt it was all somehow insignificant, although, the reality was that he was in possession of information that could be crucial to the safety of the country. He realised somebody would need notifying.

Tom clutched onto his envelope of information as if it were in danger of being snatched away from him at any moment. It was something Emily couldn't help noticing whilst walking Tom back to the stairs. 'If it's important, Mr Sharpe, I'm sure somebody else will be able to help you,' she said, gesturing at the envelope being pressed close to his chest.

'Oh, no. That's not necessary at this stage,' he replied and relaxed his vice-like grip somewhat.

Tom wanted time to think about how best to proceed from here. In this instance, he felt it would probably be best if he also got Elliott's opinion on the matter.

Walking past Dakin's old office, Tom smiled at the secretary. 'Was he quite as bad as he appeared?'

Emily only returned a diplomatic smile.

'Can I take that as a yes then?'

Beginning to open up slightly, Emily explained. 'All the other girls hated his guts. But I just saw him as a very sad, angry man who needed some help. I ended up feeling sorry for him. And really, he didn't deserve it.'

Her last sentence made Tom curious. 'So it wasn't an accident?' he asked

Emily stopped and gave him what seemed to him a confused look.

'Mr Dakin drowning. It wasn't an accident, then?' clarified Tom.

The secretary composed herself. Contrary to how she might have appeared, she hadn't been confused; her look was actually one of panic at realising what she had inadvertently just said. She gave another diplomatic smile, 'No, all I meant was it must be awful to drown. Nobody deserves that.

'Oh, I see,' responded Tom, but he sensed she was hiding something.

All the way back to the hospital Tom pondered over

the sudden death of Dakin. As was usual with him, his ruminating raised more questions than it provided answers. In the end, although he had no real foundation on which to base his thoughts, he couldn't help wondering if Dakin's investigations had disturbed something much bigger. Tom had never really thought about it much before, but the words 'secret service' now seemed very apt.

Because he was passing the coroner's office, he thought he'd check something.

Entering through the doors of the building always brought something of a shock to Tom's visual senses. On the walls were what he considered lurid green gloss tiles, stretching to two thirds of the walls' height and broken only by a thin, neat border of smaller black and white tiles. As to the area above the ceramic surface, he could never understand why anybody would choose to cover the plaster with a garish pink colour and the ceiling with a musky lemon. Even with his limited appreciation of a colour palette, he knew it looked odd. To make matters worse, the floor was constructed from tiles with a rich multi-coloured decorative pattern, which managed to confuse the visitor's sense of perspective and give the impression that he or she was trapped in a kaleidoscope.

Giving a knock on the door of Dr William Goddard's office, Tom entered. He was given the usual warm welcome by the doctor, who rose from his chair and stretched out his hand. 'Tom! How lovely to see you! Please do take a seat.'

The usual pleasantries ensued before the pair started to discuss the latest rumours of an end to hostilities by Christmas. The doctor soon dropped his head in resignation, expressing regret that he might never be able to use his medical knowledge on the front line. Tom remembered the traumatic months he'd spent grappling with the reality of being a field surgeon in Flanders and quickly reminded Goddard that there was nothing exciting about the brutal duties of the role.

Steering the conversation cleverly towards the purpose of his visit, Tom asked the doctor a favour. 'I need to know more about a man who was found drowned in the Thames a couple of days ago.'

'May I ask why?' enquired the doctor.

Tom gave an honest reply. 'Because I suspect there might have been foul play involved.'

Curious, Goddard inclined his head and moved away from the filing cabinet, which exposed a nearly empty bottle of whisky.

Tom stared at the bottle, trying to push back the memories. It was now going on two years since he had been consuming a bottle of the stuff a day and, just occasionally, his demons came back to test him. Feeling his palms becoming sweaty, he continued to glare at the bottle.

'You can have one if you like,' said Goddard.

Tom smiled appreciatively. 'No, thanks all the same, William,' he replied, knowing full well he was only ever one glass and a crisis away from reaching for the bottle again.

The doctor interrupted his thoughts. 'Would it surprise you to learn we have three or four drownings each week in London? Sometimes I've known upwards of half a dozen.'

Tom shook his head. He would have never thought it.

'Yes, drunken vagrants, desperate single mothers, fear-filled soldiers unable to take any more, and then the ones that have been … well, murdered. We get 'em all.' The doctor grabbed hold of his small collection of folders and asked, 'Your victim, male or female?'

Tom gave the doctor a description of Dakin.

'Ah, yes, here we go,' said the doctor, pulling the folder out from the others. He studied it briefly. 'That's right, bludgeoned to death.'

'So he didn't drown?' asked Tom, as the tramlines began to appear on his forehead.

'At first I thought it was drowning, but I found no water in his lungs, so that would indicate death before submersion,' confirmed the doctor. He turned the file round for Tom to see. 'This was a death caused by massive blows to the head.'

Seeing something, Goddard suddenly pulled the file back towards him and looked hard at the writing on the form. 'That's strange,' he said. 'I never wrote "death by drowning". This document seems to have been altered, Tom!'

~~~

Waiting in Major Raven's office for him to arrive, Tom picked up numerous different paintings and studied the under drawing of pencil. Leaning over the picture of Airman G. Martin, he started rubbing an eraser across the depiction of his badly disfigured cheek and missing nose. Slowly, the letters WPT began to appear. Just as he finished revealing the whole code, the door opened and in walked the major.

'Ah Tom! It seems an age since we last spoke. How are you?'

Tom grasped the major's outstretched hand and then took a seat. 'More to the point, Richard, how are you? What with all the hassle of the move.'

Finding himself quickly being dragged into troubleshooting just about every conceivable problem of the major's departmental move to Sidcup, Tom eventually diverted the conversation by telling his colleague about the death of Dakin. However, not for one minute did he think that Raven would shed a tear over the man's demise.
~~~

Having to justify his department's actions to anyone, let alone a lowly war office official, had been something the major particularly objected to.

The news about the plight of Dakin certainly didn't seem to evoke any sympathy from Raven. Instead, he simply gave a shrug of his shoulders and passed a callous comment, 'Oh well, one less idiot I have to give explanations to.'

Tom was slightly taken aback by his colleague's lack of compassion. Whilst he could share the view that Dakin had been difficult and obstructive, he couldn't accept the major's flippancy.

'I wonder if his family feel the same way, Richard?' offered Tom, his tone as cutting as one of his surgical blades.

Raven immediately got the point. 'Yes, well … perhaps I was a tad harsh. But I certainly won't be sending any flowers to his funeral.'

Tom thought it best to let the matter drop, although he now had a slightly less favourable opinion of his fellow surgeon, despite all the major's clinical brilliance.

Perhaps now wasn't the best time to mention it, but Tom felt he owed it to his departmental head to talk about why he had gone to visit Dakin. His explanation was met with dismay by the major.

'I realise you feel you acted for the best, Tom, but I'm a bit disappointed that you didn't come to me first before going to see Dakin.'

'I would have done, but you're in Sidcup so much these days,' replied Tom, although he knew that if he were honest, his efforts to make contact with Raven hadn't exactly been rigorous. He'd known that his colleague would have insisted on coming along, and that could have proved disastrous.

Reluctantly, Major Raven had to agree that Tom was right. In the last week, he'd only visited the hospital on three brief occasions. The rest of the time he was out preparing for his department's forthcoming move. Giving a nonchalant shake of his head in acceptance of the facts, he asked, 'So what is it exactly that you've discovered?'

Tom began to explain things from the very beginning. Raven listened with increasing interest, lifting his eyebrows occasionally in amazement at the audacity of it all.

'And you've checked some paintings to test the theory?'

Tom pointed over to the watercolours lying on the desk. 'That's what I was doing when you came in. Look at the one for the airman.'

Raven picked up the painting to see the code WPT7365 clearly visible within the destruction of the man's face. 'Good God!' he cried. Continuing to look at the code, it took a moment before he carried on. 'Have you challenged Wilson?'

'That's not my job, Richard. Hence my visit to Dakin.'

'Yes of course,' agreed Raven. 'Listen, Tom. I know people we can take this to. People that I trust! Let me make some calls and come back to you.'

Tom didn't have a problem with the suggestion. To some extent, he would be relieved to pass the whole thing over, now that the puzzle had been solved.

With Tom gone, Raven picked up the telephone. 'Yes, operator, connect me to Colonel Coniston at Whitehall 9291 ... Hello, it's Raven. We have a problem. A very big problem!'

Chapter 24

Sitting on his usual rendezvous bench on the Embankment, Colonel Coniston turned over the page of his newspaper and allowed it to drop at one corner so he could have a clear view towards the river. The stout officer pushed out his chest, and his chin protruded upwards as if his collar was too tight. His peppery grey walrus moustache rose up at the ends. It all made him look terribly pompous; but then that's exactly what he was.

The arrival of a large woman directly in front of him suddenly blocked his view in all directions.

'Excuse me, madam. If I had wanted a view of an overweight backside, I would have paid for it!' said the colonel, his rudeness being second only to his arrogance, and always incongruous with his position.

The woman turned around, aghast. 'Really! How dare —' she started to say indignantly, but before she had time to finish, the colonel spotted the person he had been waiting for in the distance and hastily got up to leave. The woman was left standing flabbergasted.

At the riverside, the colonel came to a standstill beside

a man looking down at a pleasure boat approaching the pier. 'Bloody sightseers!' he moaned.

The man pulled himself upright. It was Major Raven. 'A fine morning,' he commented.

'Is it?' the colonel replied, his mouth dropping to give him the look of a fish. He quickly got round to business. 'So, it seems we have somebody sticking their oar in where it's not needed. Tell me about him.'

Raven duly gave as much detail of Tom as he could and, more importantly, explained how his colleague had discovered the code in the paintings.

'Well, that's all we damned well need,' spat the colonel. 'First a department detective starts to meddle. And now some amateur do-gooder professor comes on the scene. We need to get rid of him.'

The colonel stared out over the river, contemplating the options.

'We can't just get rid of him,' stated Raven. 'Tom Sharpe is well respected and very popular. The hospital board would start an investigation, I'm sure. We don't want that. And if things were made to look like an accident, the hospital would ask the coroner for a full autopsy. Again, do we want that? Perhaps it would be better to just let me try and stall him, if you could arrange to pull the date forward.'

Continuing to stare at the water, the colonel took his time before responding. 'Or we simply turn the tables and have the professor arrested for suspected espionage. I could have intelligence staff crawling all over him with just a couple of calls. All you'd need to do would be to ensure they found something damning.'

'But he'll divulge how the code is done,' protested the major, looking confused.

'Yes he will, but to a person that I control. Don't worry I can introduce enough red tape to buy extra time for everything in our arrangement to be finished properly.'

It was a risky strategy and one which might prove a disaster, but the colonel was confident that his level of authority would make it work. He knew that by the time the police finally discovered that Tom was telling the truth, everybody would be long gone.

When it came to framing Tom, Raven realised it might prove easier than he thought. Tom's interest in facial surgery had meant he'd already taken a small collection of paintings to his office. All that was now needed was for the major to carefully place some secret documents and valuable information amongst the paperwork strewn all over his colleague's desk. Everything else then slotted perfectly into place because, just like the major, his fellow surgeon had access to the medical bags going out to France. He also knew Wilson, and he was privy to lots of medical advances that could benefit the enemy. This would surely show Tom as being fully involved.

Certainly there was enough evidence available for any diligent investigator to make an arrest.

~~~

Tom was leaving the theatre with Green after a particularly grueling morning's work when Major Raven, accompanied by a police constable and a man dressed in a dark brown suit, approached them. From the serious look on Raven's face, it was immediately clear there was a problem.

'Richard, whatever is wrong?' asked Tom.

Raven said nothing, his facial expression never altering from one of obvious disappointment.

'What?' Tom urged.

Moments later, the suited man stated his intention, much to the utter surprise, not only of Tom, but also of Green.

'Professor Thomas Sharpe, I am arresting you on suspicion of espionage. You don't have to say —'

'Now just wait a minute,' interrupted Tom, flinging off the constable's hand from his arm. But it was to no avail. The man, obviously someone with authority, carried on reading Tom his rights, whilst the constable took a much firmer grip on his arm and placed him in handcuffs.

'Richard! What is this all about?' cried Tom.

'I can't help you. They've found it all.'
~~~

'Found what?'

Tom struggled to keep turning round as he was led away. 'Found what? Where?' he kept repeating. 'Richard! For God's sake answer me.'

He didn't.

Watching Tom as he was dragged out of sight, a thoroughly perplexed Green turned to Raven and demanded to know. 'What the hell is going on?'

'The colonel's idea,' replied the major. He paused for a second. 'Sharpe's discovered the code.'

'What!'

Raven briefly explained the colonel's plan.

Green couldn't believe things were happening without his knowledge. Throughout all his dealings with his accomplices in the arrangement, Green had always been consulted on the decisions.

'And when was I suddenly excluded from having any say in the arrangement?' snarled Green.

Spreading out his hands, Raven shrugged. 'Speak with Coniston.'

Although Green was Steinhauer's golden protégé, he couldn't help believing he was now being doubled crossed and thought that, in his case, 'long gone' would actually mean 'long dead'.

~~~
~~~

Once in custody, and as the questioning continued, it didn't take long for Tom to realise that he was being very cleverly set up. But why, he thought? He didn't want to believe that his friend, Major Raven, had any part in the whole affair. Instead he preferred to think of the major as simply being genuinely shocked and disappointed at what had been found in his office. But his experience of helping Elliott on his case files had also taught him that people often had two very different sides to them. He sat considering the possibilities until it occurred to him – the very same reasons why he appeared as a prime suspect for espionage also applied to Raven.

Time and time again, Tom explained to his interrogator that he had no idea why secret and sensitive information had been found on his desk. And time and time again, he was called a liar. The plain truth – that he had just worked out the code – seemed to be falling on deaf ears. To have any chance, Tom realised he had to change tack. 'I refuse to answer any more questions without legal representation,' he said with defiance, although, he had little or no idea of who might represent him. The last time he'd had need of a solicitor was for the conveyancing involved in his house purchase. The obvious then came to mind: who better to help and guide him than Elliott! However, the logistics of getting a visit in his police station cell from a friend who was currently lying in a hospital bed with one leg up to his groin in plaster might prove a challenge.

Tom was finally left alone in his cell, without food or water. He slumped down exhausted. It was now nearing four o'clock in the afternoon and, in addition to having performed five hours of surgery, he had had to endure three hours of arduous questioning. His thoughts turned to Mary. He needed to let her know of his plight.

Unknown to Tom, however, that problem, had already been taken care of. Nathan Green had boarded the 4.45 tube train bound for Finsbury Park.

~~~

With baby Lucinda asleep, Mary felt she could have heard a pin drop. It all seemed strange. One day the house had been full of people and activity, the next it was empty and deathly quiet. Sitting in the kitchen, she poured herself a cup of tea and savoured the peace and solitude. A sudden knock on the door made her jump up, spilling her tea. 'Damn and blast,' she cursed, quickly trying to mop it up with a tea towel.

Opening the front door, Mary was totally surprised to see the man who had been Tom's dinner guest. 'Oh! Hello, Mr Green. I certainly wasn't expecting it to be you.'

'Hello, Mrs Sharpe.' Green tipped his hat. 'Might I have a word?'
~~~

'Er … well, yes.'

Mary wasn't really sure what to think, but stood to one side and held out her hand to invite him in. Her instinct was still to always show courtesy and trust towards people, despite her experience of being tricked and held captive years earlier.

'Please,' said Mary, leading the way into the parlour.

Green followed, transfixed by Mary's silken hair tucked up in a thick bun. He wondered if it was actually parted in the middle when let down. Perhaps she simply wore it pushed back. Catching her eye and enjoying her subsequent gentle smile, he briefly wondered whether he could really kill someone he'd dreamt so long about loving. A woman who was not only beautiful, but also so graceful and elegant. He fought hard to think logically; even if it had been possible for him to murder Tom and then befriend Mary over time, would she ever have loved him in the way he wanted? His warped mind produced the consoling thought that what he was going to do would provide him with a permanent reminder of her.

Green now had three days before the last mattresses went to France. He had so much to do, but the most important item was to get Mary to board the train and meet him in Peterborough. Everything else surrounding Wilson, Mrs Sowerby and Daniel, he could control. That was simply a case of loading his gun with three bullets once he had what he wanted – the last codes.

'So what is it that I can help you with, Mr Green?' asked Mary, interrupting his contemplation.

Green spoke plainly. 'It's Tom. I'm afraid he's been arrested.'

'Arrested!' Mary was stunned. It took a moment for the statement to fully sink in. Eventually she was able to ask, 'For what reason, exactly, Mr Green?'

Like some accomplished repertory actor, Green took a dramatic pause before answering. 'I'm sorry to tell you, Mrs Sharpe, he's being held on suspicion of carrying out espionage activities.'

Mary just couldn't believe it and began to laugh. 'Tom arrested for spying! Don't be ridiculous.'

Green gave a shrug of his shoulders. 'It's true, I'm afraid.' He watched as Mary's amusement slowly turned to alarm.

'But how can it be true? Tom would never betray his country.' Mary's Irish lilt became more pronounced as her anxiety grew. She took stock. 'No, it simply can't be right. There must be some mistake.'

Green took great pleasure in shaking his head before going on to explain the details of what had happened, and using every opportunity to show his pretended sympathy.

'If there's anything I can do to help, Mrs Sharpe?'

Mary stood by the mantelpiece, her hands clutched together tightly. The anxious look on her face fuelled

Green's intention to make the most out of the crisis. He was, however, taken aback by a sudden change in Mary's attitude. 'Well, I'd better get down to the police station and try and help get to the bottom of this nonsense.'

Green was thrown by his hostess's pragmatic approach. He had expected Mary to quickly become a quivering wreck; but then he didn't know just how strong the woman in front of him could be. The anxious expression on her face was suddenly replaced by one of determination.

'I thank you immensely for coming all this way to inform me of my husband's unfortunate situation, Mr Green, but if you'll now excuse me, I must make a couple of telephone calls.'

'Er … yes, indeed,' muttered Green, rising from his chair. 'Perhaps I could call in on you later and provide some further help?' he attempted.

'It's very kind of you, but I'm sure that won't be necessary.'

Mary's confidence and ability to deal with things angered the doctor. When talking with women, even with most men, he was used to dominating and controlling matters. In future, he realised he would need to be more persuasive. Giving a forced smile, he walked towards the front door and, just as he was ready to leave, baby Lucinda started to cry out from upstairs.

'What about your daughter, Mrs Sharpe? Who will look after her whilst you visit Tom?'

Mary hadn't thought about it, assuming she would just be allowed to take her baby with her to into the police station. 'Well … I hadn't —'

'If it becomes a problem,' interrupted Green, seeing an opportunity to take back control. 'I have a sister who I'm sure would be more than happy to help look after her for short periods.'

'Oh! That's very kind. I might just take you up on that.'

Another staged grin spread across Green's face. 'Well, good luck with Tom. And rest assured I'll be doing all I can to get the hospital board involved. Don't forget, anything I can do … anything at all.'

'Thank you, Mr Green.'

Tom's colleague tipped his hat. 'Please, do call me Nathan.'

Chapter 25

Until the last couple of days, Daniel's experiences of London had only been pleasurable ones. Now his little world had come crashing down. Nothing that was happening to him seemed to be part of a set order any more. He was no longer in familiar surroundings. It was all having a traumatic effect, causing him to rock his body and tap his head more often and for longer than was usual. Even with all her experience of dealing with Daniel, Mrs Sowerby was now struggling to keep him reassured. But, despite the desperateness of the situation, she knew she had to try and establish a routine.

What was needed was to get the boy to immerse himself once more in his fantasy world of General Custer and his troops; but without his toy figures, this was difficult. Eventually, Mrs Sowerby managed to get him to start reciting the different battles. However, she couldn't help noticing how unusually violent and graphic he was making his descriptions. It didn't take long for her to realise that Daniel's behaviour was a direct reaction to being roughly handled by Green. Whilst their conversation about the General might have achieved the goal of providing Daniel with familiarity, Mrs Sowerby had to stop when the disturbed boy began to re-enact the killing of a cavalryman by the Sioux.

Out of breath, Daniel slumped down. He asked the same question he'd asked at least fifty times already that morning, 'When is Peter coming?'

'Maybe this afternoon or tonight,' Mrs Sowerby repeated yet again, desperately hoping this might be true.

The bare room where the couple were being held was on the upper level of an empty warehouse. It was furnished with nothing more than a few flattened cardboard boxes, some hessian sacks, and a bucket to be used for ablutions. On an upturned wooden crate in the centre was a handful of spent candles; and leaning on top of the door frame was a metal 'Exit' sign, which at some stage had been left there. High across one wall was a row of small windows which allowed in plenty of brightness during the day and the glow of a street gas lamp at night.

In an attempt to keep up their spirits, Mrs Sowerby decided to play a game of hand slap. She giggled as more often than not she managed to get her hands out of the way of Daniel's sweeping palm. 'Ah ha!' she laughed out each time she succeeded.

The ring of her laughter was broken by the sound of footsteps on the wooden floor of the corridor. Mrs

Sowerby dropped her hands and waited. Sure enough, the key turned in the lock and the door opened. In stepped Green, his words matching his contemptuous look.

'Get up!'

'Are we free to go?' asked Mrs Sowerby, with a glimmer of hope.

The resulting disdainful snort told her the answer.

Daniel tried to edge behind his nurse, not wishing to make any eye contact with Green. From the back of his mind came his memories. He studied the face of the doctor hard. Images of the gauze being put over his face, followed by waking up underneath the tarpaulin, kept flashing in front of him.

The boy then gasped in terror as Green produced a revolver and aimed it at Mrs Sowerby. 'Right, you come with me!'

'But what about —'

'He stays here.'

Mrs Sowerby looked up at Green, her eyes almost pleading. She edged her fingers behind her back, seeking out Daniel's hand. 'He's just a boy, sir, and right now he needs me more than ever.'

Green showed not a modicum of understanding. Instead he just repeated, forcefully, 'He stays here!'

Turning quickly to look Daniel directly in the eye, Mrs Sowerby clasped both his hands. 'Listen to me. I have to go out for a while, but I'll be back as soon as —'

'No!' shouted Daniel.

Mrs Sowerby drew his hands towards her. 'I have to, sweetheart. Just for a while.' She paused and looked back at Green, who gave a single nod indicating that she should hurry up. Slowly, she released the boy's hands. 'Can you start thinking about all the places in London we've recently been to and put them into the order we saw them … there was Nelson's Column and …'

But Daniel just stared ahead.

Mrs Sowerby pleaded again with Green. 'Wherever it is we're going, I promise he'll be no trouble.'

The uncompromising Green grabbed her arm and pushed her towards the door.

Once more the boy began rocking.

Hearing him suddenly begin to recite the landmarks, Mrs Sowerby tried to wedge herself in the door frame and shouted out encouragement. 'That's it, Daniel! Then there was the Portrait Gallery, the Haymarket …'

Green slammed his fist down hard on her arm, forcing her to release her grip on the architrave. The next moment the door was closed and locked behind her.

As they moved down the corridor, Daniel's muffled voice could still be heard reciting the list. Eventually, he paused, and then started all over again. 'Nelson's column …'

And, that was how he carried on for the next hour,

until, for no particular reason, he suddenly stopped and felt in his pocket. Pulling out a small envelope, he tipped Mary's rings into his hands. For some time he studied them, until, eventually, he gave each one a name and was soon at play with the 7th Cavalry.

~~~

Green and Mrs Sowerby said virtually nothing to each other as they travelled to the Strand Palace Hotel. It was only as they approached the entrance that he pulled back on her arm and spoke. His words and grip left the housekeeper in no doubt that if she tried anything silly he would kill her. To emphasize his point, Green pushed the revolver, which was concealed under his folded overcoat, deep into her side.

Knowing she might already be on borrowed time, Elsie Sowerby had no intention of trying to escape. Even if she did have a chance, she wouldn't put Daniel at any more risk than he already was.

Green's instructions were quite simple: posing as guests they would make their way to the telephone booths. Once there, he would speak with the operator and then Wilson. After that, on his signal, she would be allowed a brief few words with the artist. He finished by reminding her of what would happen if she tried any nonsense.
~~~

Although alone in the studio, Wilson knew he was still highly visible and told himself that when the call came he needed to act as if everything was normal. However, when the phone did finally ring, he just snatched at it, moving as quickly as if he were catching a tumbling glass of water. 'Hello!' he cried, taking the operator by surprise at the speed with which he picked up.

'You're connected now caller.'

'Well, Arthur,' said Green. 'Have you done them?'

The highly anxious Wilson took a deep breath, trying hard not to show his immediate disappointment that the voice on the line wasn't that of Elsie. 'Yes, I've done them, but why are there three?'

'You needn't worry yourself about that.'

Never before had Wilson known more than one coded painting to be dispatched at a time. The fact that three were suddenly going to be sent at once had told him something new or different was happening. But what was so large that it needed three mattresses?

'And are you finding the call interesting, operator?' Green asked calmly. He had no real idea whether the young woman was still connected, but it was a ploy that usually rid the line of a nosey and opportunist operator listening in. On this occasion, he was right, and the young woman in the exchange hastily pulled out her cord and looked nervously towards the supervisor standing on a rostrum behind her.

'Is Elsie there?' Wilson demanded.

'Yes.'

'And Daniel?'

'She'll confirm he's fine.'

Green handed over the stand of the candlestick telephone to Elsie, but kept hold of the ear piece. Leaning forward, he carefully placed it between both their ears. Elsie Sowerby had already been terrified. Having Green almost breathing down her neck made her even more so.

'Hello,' said Elsie, nervously.

Wilson felt the adrenaline rush to his stomach. 'Elsie.'

'Oh Peter!' she cried, hardly able to breathe. 'Please, please do exactly what he wants!'

'Which do I like best, a cake or a biscuit?' Wilson all at once asked.

'What?'

'Tell me, Elsie, which?'

Wilson knew his fellow agent only too well and needed to be convinced the voice he was hearing wasn't that of another woman acting Elsie's part.

'A biscuit,' confirmed a perplexed Elsie.

All Wilson's fears suddenly disappeared. 'I'm coming to get you as soon as I can.'

Elsie couldn't help sobbing. 'Be careful, Peter,' she managed.

'Daniel. How is Daniel?'

'He's fine.'

'I love you, Elsie. Be brave.'

Green grabbed hold of the phone mouthpiece. 'Aaah! So touching. You'll have me crying next.'

Wilson felt his anger rise. He gritted his teeth. 'If anything happens to them, I swear I'll —'

'Shall we just stick to what we agreed, eh,' interrupted Green. 'Take the tube to Aldgate East and meet me on the corner of Leman Street at 7 o'clock.'

Before he could say anything further, the artist heard the sound of the line disconnecting. He cursed and threw down the earpiece, angry that once again, Green was able to have everything on his own terms. Rubbing his tense brow, he accepted that for now that was how things would have to be.

When Mrs Sowerby was taken back to the warehouse, she found Daniel curled up, fast asleep. Not wanting to wake him, she just sat down with her back resting against the wall and gently stroked his hair. The boy's tear-stained cheeks confirmed her fears that during her absence he had become anxious and upset. 'I'm back now, my darling, I'm back. There's no more need to worry,' she softly murmured, though she had no idea whether her words would prove to be true. She closed her eyes, but despite being exhausted, she was unable to do more than doze on and off for about an hour. She was far too apprehensive about what was going to happen next. What had happened to Peter, she wondered. By eight o'clock that evening she had her answer.

~~~

With a folder of pictures under his left arm, Wilson cautiously approached Leman Street. He could see Green straight ahead, at the entrance to a side alley. Each man had a coat draped over his right arm, beneath which he fixed the other with a silenced pistol.

When they were finally standing in front of each other, Wilson indicated his folder, from which the three paintings protruded. Green gave a nod and they slowly edged into the alley, still brandishing their guns. Wilson was the first to speak, 'After three?'

Green raised his brow in agreement.

'One … two … three!'

As was the agreed procedure in these situations, each man broke open his gun and emptied the chamber of bullets onto the floor. With the swipe of a foot, the shells were sent sliding across the tarmac, making a distinctive clinking sound. Then came the most dangerous part of the process, frisking each other for more weapons. Each knew that at any stage he could be double crossed and
~~~

attacked by the other, although Wilson was confident he could win if it came down to simply throwing punches. Tentatively, the two did their searches and pulled apart, each nodding to indicate the other was clean.

Nevertheless, Wilson remained on his guard. He knew there was no trusting Green.

Although the sound of approaching footsteps filled Mrs Sowerby with dread, it was also her only hope of being set free. Assuming the door would soon be unlocked, she shook Daniel to wake him and hoped he wouldn't react badly. Luckily, he didn't. He just opened his eyes and stared around. Eventually, he simply asked, 'When is Peter coming?'

What long term effect the whole experience would have on Daniel, Mrs Sowerby could only guess at; but for now she had to concentrate on the present. Getting to her feet, she held his hand tight, praying she would not be forced to leave him again.

To her relief and delight, as the door opened she saw Wilson. 'Peter!' she cried, and started to rush forward, but pulled up abruptly as Green came into view. Instinctively, Daniel had moved behind her for protection. Seeing his friend standing next to the man he associated with bad things confused him. He gave no reaction to Mrs Sowerby saying, 'Look, it's Peter. I told you he would come.'

Wilson glanced around the room, looking for anything

that might suggest Green would have the opportunity to double cross him. The room was so empty he couldn't possibly see how he could be deceived.

As both men edged into the room, all Elsie Sowerby wanted to do was run towards Wilson and hug him, but she realised that some agreed procedure was taking place. Nervously, she watched as Green took the keys out of the door and stood aside. 'Shall we?'

On the count of three Green threw the keys across the floor towards the wall, whilst Wilson slid his folder with the three paintings back towards the door. Only then did the artist drop his guard and beckon Elsie to him. She fell into his arms sobbing, 'Oh Peter, thank God, you're here.'

Slowly, Daniel walked forwards, unsure what exactly was expected of him. Awkwardly, he held out his arms and tried to cuddle them.

None of them had noticed Green reaching up to the 'Exit' sign and carefully moving it aside, before pulling down a revolver. 'You're a bigger fool than I ever imagined, Wilson,' he sneered and pointed the barrel at his opponent's chest.

Wilson was mortified, yet he had to agree he had been a fool. Just one momentary lapse in concentration had put everyone back in danger. Frantically, he racked his brains. But what could he do? Realistically there wasn't anything. Elsie dropped her head in desperation.

Daniel, however, was standing with his eyes locked on the revolver. All that was going through his mind was an association between the gun and the possibility of him being left alone. The thought terrified him. He started to twitch and felt the dampness on his leg. Then Custer's voice from his play acting began ringing in his head. 'For God's sake be still, boy! You're part of the United States 7th Cavalry. Stand up and fight!'

With eyes as wide as a startled deer, Daniel launched himself forwards. Green reacted by spinning round and re-directing his aim.

'Daniel!' screamed Elsie. But it was too late; the boy had leapt as far as he could and was now bearing down on the gun. Green squeezed the trigger.

The bodies thudded to the ground. Elsie gasped and turned her head into Wilson's chest. There was a brief moment of silence and disbelief at what Daniel had done.

Elsie cried 'Nooooo! and fled to the boy's side. But she was stunned to see him lift up his body and begin to rain down punches on Green.

By the grace of God Green's revolver had jammed and was now lying some yards away.

Wilson reacted quickly and got to the gun before Green. The doctor was finally able to land a punch on Daniel that knocked him out cold; but with his slight frame he struggled to push the dead weight of the boy's body off his own. By the time he did manage it, Wilson had grabbed him by the throat and was pressing the gun against his temple. Uncocking and recocking it in the hope of clearing the jam, he fired a test shot into the corridor. The loud bang made Elsie gasp and cringe.

Wilson turned the gun back towards Green's head, his finger firmly hugging the contour of the trigger. 'Say a prayer, you evil —'

'No!' shouted Elsie. 'No, please, Peter, don't. This is not what I want. Please do not shoot him. I couldn't bear the thought of you killing someone.'

With gritted teeth, Wilson was looking at Green with hatred. He smashed his clenched fist across the doctor's face. 'Elsie, trust me he's evil.'

Elsie had by now knelt down and was cradling Daniel in her arms. 'I know, I've witnessed it first hand, but —'

'He deserves to die.'

'Let a judge decide that, Peter, please.'

She had to turn away as Wilson began smashing Green's skull against the floor boards. Eventually, with his victim totally unconscious, he stopped and spat at him. 'Scum!'

What had been a traumatic succession of days was finally over. Wilson took off his jacket, placed it over Elsie shoulders and then picked up Daniel to carry him.

Turning the key in the lock with Green inside the room allowed Elsie to give a huge sigh of relief. The next time she placed a key in a door couldn't have been more different. That evening was spent in a family room in a West End hotel.

Chapter 26

Mary still couldn't accept that Tom had got mixed up in something related to spying. She could, however, well believe her husband might have involved himself in something which he considered totally innocent, but which anyone else would have realised might have dangerous consequences. That was Tom through and through. How many times had Mary played devil's advocate, arguing that his actions could be misinterpreted, and might have an adverse effect on how people saw him? But, she could never have imagined what was happening now.

To help her make sense of it all Mary turned to the two people she trusted implicitly – the Elliotts. These were people she knew not just as dear friends but almost as parents. In all her past troubles, it was they who had helped her through her darkest times. Ann, always Mary's emotional support and shoulder to cry on, had instantly offered to catch the next train to London in order to help in any way she could; but they both knew it was Elliott, with all his experience of the judicial system, who was best placed to advise her. The trouble with Elliott's advice, though, was that it usually went hand in hand with his direct involvement.

After listening to her friend explaining the whole story of the pictures, Daniel's reaction to them, and how, ultimately, that had led him and Tom to discover the codes, Mary was still confused as to why her husband should be arrested. Elliott was more astute: he suspected the whole affair might be part of something much bigger, and that Tom was now being used as a distraction. He knew he needed to get down to the police station where Tom was being held as soon as possible.

Sister Lucas's discussion with Elliott about him wanting to leave the hospital was an interesting one. 'Mr Elliott, might I remind you this isn't a hotel where you can just wander in and out at your pleasure. You have a broken femur and need bed rest, contrary to what you might think!'

Elliott took no real notice and carried on trying to gather together his clothes.

'I must insist you get back into bed immediately, Mr Elliott,' cried the sister, although her words were shouted more in hope than with any certainty that her patient would comply.

Nothing was going very well for the sister this morning. Not only had Tom not arrived for work, but also neither had Green. She hadn't heard a word from either man and, as a consequence, the whole theatre department was now thrown into disarray.

'I'm afraid this is my entire fault, sister, or, more accurately, that of my husband,' stated Mary, with some embarrassment.

'And may I enquire who exactly you are, madam?' answered the sister, her frustration beginning to get the better of her.

'I'm Mary Sharpe. Professor Sharpe's wife.'

'Oh! I see,' said the shocked sister, and then gave Mary an apologetic look. 'You said this was the fault of your husband. Is Professor Sharpe in some kind of trouble?'

'You haven't been told?'

'No.'

Mary began to explain as Elliott wheeled himself away to get dressed.

~~~

Aided by Mary, Elliott battled his way across the city and finally arrived at the police station. Little did the staff there realise what was about to hit them. For the last few years, their only experience of a probation officer had been of a rather docile, indecisive man who commanded little respect for the role. He had certainly only ever exerted minimal influence with his appearances in court.
~~~

And most of the time in the police station, his opinion was simply ignored, especially by the duty sergeant. It therefore came as a shock to the sergeant when he was suddenly interrogated vigorously by Elliott about his friend's incarceration. Nevertheless he stood his ground.

Realising he wasn't getting anywhere, Elliott decided it was time for a bit of bluff, and started peppering his speech with references to legal requirements for the handling of prisoners. For some of his references, he could only remember the briefest of details; but Elliott had one thing in abundance – a commanding presence. Even when hobbling on crutches.

The station staff watched in amazement as Elliott soon began running rings around their sergeant, reciting one procedure after another and occasionally throwing in a reference to an offender's rights under the 'Probation of Offenders Act, 1907'. Even when the sergeant thought Elliott had got it wrong, he was uneasy about saying as much because the man in front of him was so convincing with his knowledge.

'… And therefore, sergeant, by the power invested in me by the said act, I demand to see Mr Sharpe without further delay,' concluded Elliott, wondering whether he'd gone a step too far.

Of course, it was all nonsense. Elliott had no power whatsoever in a London police station; but the sergeant, who was by now ready to explode with irritation, decided to give in. He did, however, draw the line at allowing Mary access to the cells. The prisoner's wife would have to wait until visiting was allowed, 'And that,' he stated, 'could be some days yet.' A dejected Mary reluctantly agreed to return home and await further news.

'Constable McCauley,' said the sergeant, beckoning a young officer towards him. 'Show Mr Elliott to Mr Sharpe's cell. And, as our visitor has pointed out, it wouldn't be unreasonable for him to be offered a cup of tea. Please arrange something.'

The reluctant constable led the way to the cells before sarcastically remarking, 'And would sir like sugar?'

'Yes, five spoonfuls,' Elliott answered, not batting an eyelid.

'Five!' spluttered the constable in amazement.

Elliott was on top form with his quips. 'Yes, but don't stir it. I don't like it too sweet.'

At last he was able to enter the small, dirty and fusty-smelling cell. Tom was more grateful to see him than Elliott could have imagined. He thanked his old friend for coming, and optimistically waited for guidance.

'Yes, well. All I've done is bluffed my way in to see you, Tom. As soon as they find out that there's no such thing as Section 5 Appendix (d), I'm afraid I'll be out on my ear. But hopefully by then we will have got you some proper representation. Mary tells me you don't have a solicitor.'

'No, not really.'

'Umm, then I'll see if Ernest Cooper can recommend someone,' said Elliott, trying not to grimace at the pain of constantly hobbling about.

'You really shouldn't be out on that leg.'

'I know, I know.' Elliott waved his hand in dismissal.

The pair had just started discussing their options when a set of keys jangled in the lock. The door opened, and a man dressed in military uniform entered. 'Mr Sharpe.' he said decisively. '...and Mr Elliott, I believe?'

The next five minutes of conversation were very enlightening.

The army officer introduced himself as Brigadier Armstrong from the War Office, explaining that he was responsible for a counter espionage investigation that went deep into the heart of Whitehall. The officer wouldn't elaborate as to the exact details, but did confirm that Tom had indeed been framed. What was more interesting was the brigadier's information that the codes had actually been discovered some time ago. The secret service, however, had decided to play along with the leaking of secrets in the hope of flushing out more of the people it had under surveillance. The prize fish they were hoping to reel in were a high-ranking officer and a member of the serving cabinet, neither of whom he would name.

Tom naturally wanted to know who had set him up. The answer, which hinted very strongly at Major Raven and his protégé, Nathan Green, totally staggered him. In all the time he had worked with the pair, never had Tom suspected either of being a traitor. Elliott for his part was simply interested to learn how the officer knew his own name and his whereabouts. The answers given were barely enough to satisfy his curiosity, but it was obvious the brigadier was not prepared to reveal much more about his department's methods.

The continuing discussion established that Tom and Elliott had discovered the codes just as the brigadier's team was poised to strike and make arrests. As outsiders, their involvement quickly began to present a significant risk to the whole operation, and now, with Coniston having Tom arrested, things had become critical. An official need for silence meant the pair either had to be told certain details and used in the operation or their disappearance had to be arranged. Fortunately, the service favoured the former.

Agreeing that Tom should be detained for another couple of days so as not to raise any suspicion, the brigadier confirmed he would then arrange to have it seem as though Tom was being released on bail. After that, the expectation was that Tom would start passing false information to Raven and Green. As for Elliott, he would simply be required to support his friend wherever possible.

However, what the brigadier had not yet received intelligence about was the timescale Coniston was working to as he organized the sending of the last mattresses. If he and his colleagues did not receive this information very soon, in two days' time there would be no one left to arrest.

That afternoon a stroke of good luck was to come Brigadier Armstrong's way, when one of his contacts brought him some information that had been discovered concerning Wilson's plans. If he worked quickly and skillfully, the brigadier knew he had a perfect opportunity to bring the whole affair to a swift conclusion.

Chapter 27

Coming round from unconsciousness, Green's instinct was to try and get to his feet, but he was forced to first sit up and get his bearings. The splitting pain in his head, from Wilson constantly banging it against the floor, was almost unbearable. He dragged himself to the wall, and leant back, cursing the situation he now found himself in.

Eventually, he struggled to his feet, but had to slump back down and then began vomiting. His concussion was worse than he thought. All his medical knowledge was telling him that he had to just close his eyes and relax for a while. It took a good ten minutes before he felt able to attempt getting to his feet again.

At last stable, Green tried the door. Why, he wasn't sure. Really it was just instinct. Not for one minute did he believe Wilson would have left it unlocked. He was right.

With his thoughts becoming more coherent, he glanced around searching for options to escape. Realistically there were only: either try to barge the door down, though considering it was solid beech and opened inwards, this would prove an almost impossible task; or to try and get to the high window. Whilst this would be the better option, it was still not an easy one. The window was only tiny and positioned at least eight feet from the floor.

Green figured that if he stacked the ablution bucket on top of the crate, he should be able to reach the ledge. Even then, it would still need almighty strength to pull up his body and anchor his leg in place. However, when faced with the alternative of perishing, the battered doctor knew he had to try. He made three attempts, all to no avail. The physical strength needed was beyond him, and particularly in his fragile state. Once again, he slumped to the floor and closed his eyes. For a moment he doubted whether he could achieve it. Perhaps it would be best to just sleep for a while and try again later. Yet he knew he might have some serious damage to his head and, with each hour that passed, he might get weaker and weaker.

For a man so used to being in control, he now looked a desperate wreck, pathetically holding his head in his hands. Just as his eyes were forcing themselves closed, he had an idea. He shot upright. 'You idiot!' he called out. 'Why didn't you think of it earlier?'

Holding up his foot, Green then crashed it down onto the crate. As he hoped, it cracked the wooden slats. Pulling at one, he managed to tear it from the structure whilst still keeping its nails in place. Now, with a makeshift pick, the reinvigorated doctor began to hack away at the plaster on the wall. Within the hour he had created enough holes to form a climbing route.

Once he reached the window ledge, it didn't take long for him to kick through the glass and then begin to squeeze himself out. Luckily for Green, the roof guttering was near enough for him to grab hold of. From there it was a case of carefully edging his way across a course of protruding decorative bricks towards a fire escape.

Finally, Green reached out and firmly pulled himself onto the cast iron stairway. He collapsed exhausted. Against the odds he had managed to escape.

Waiting to build his strength once again, the doctor began thinking what to do. What previously had been straightforward was now problematic. There were so many questions that needed answers. Why hadn't Wilson just killed him? Would he have betrayed him to the authorities yet? Would it be safe to go home? Had the mattresses been sent? How much time did he have?

One thing about which he was resolute was that his trip to Peterborough and the operation on his sister would not be affected. Maude was already staying at a hotel there, awaiting her brother's arrival, which supposedly would happen after he had confirmed everything had gone to plan with the arrangement. The whole of his and Maude's future relied on that.

Of course then came the biggest question of all: how was

he going to convince Mary to catch the train with him to Peterborough?

<div align="center">~~~</div>

Elsie tensed at the gentle knock on the door. Nervously, she stepped over towards it and leant her head forward. 'Hello,' she said quietly.

'Elsie, it's me,' came the whispered reply.

'Oh Peter!' cried Elsie with relief, and swiftly opened the door. 'Thank the lord you're back.'

Wilson stood in front of her clutching a bottle of champagne and two glasses.

An anxious Elsie looked at him in disbelief. 'Where on earth have you been? You said you wouldn't be longer than an hour. You've been out for over four!'

'Yes, sorry. Things took a little longer than I anticipated, but everything is sorted out now.'

What that really meant was that he'd done something with the mattresses.

Wilson had easy access to the hospital stores, and he knew the processes and procedures very well. Prior to working in the art studio with Raven, he had worked in the dispatch department, and therefore had knowledge of exactly what forms would need to be amended to re-route the mattresses. And with all his skill in preparing artwork, he was quite at home making any alterations required.

Working with care and precision, he had skillfully deleted the three relevant mattresses from the dispatch sheet for France and listed them as faulty returns. Then all that had been needed was for him to cunningly amend the returns label and send them to the residential address of a corrupt contact. The only potential problem was whether the contact would honor his agreement to send them on to a storage company for him. Wilson could only hope that the amount of money he'd paid him, and his explanation that the mattresses were stolen goods, would be enough to ensure the man's cooperation.

Wilson gave a mysterious smile of satisfaction and held up the bottle. 'Come, I want us to celebrate.'

Elsie pulled away from the outstretched arm he was trying to put round her shoulder. 'I've been worried sick. What has taken so long? And what do you mean by sorted out?'

It was the first time Wilson had seen Elsie so insistent. With determination, she spelled out her wish to get to the bottom of the situation. 'Peter, if we're to have a future, there can't be any secrets, no deceit or lies between us.'

He watched as she gestured towards the door that led into the room where Daniel was still asleep. 'I have a responsibility towards that boy in there. To ensure he's safe and properly cared for. I can't put him at risk.'

Walking over to the window, she pulled back the net

curtain and looked down towards the street. 'You say things are sorted out for now. But what about tomorrow and the day after, then the day after that? Will there be more secrets then? Who will I be able to trust?' She carefully allowed the curtain to fall out of her hand before turning back to look at Wilson, 'I need you to be honest with me, Peter, and tell me exactly what is going on.' The emotion in her voice could not disguise an element of firmness.

Wilson was not used to being spoken to by a woman in such a direct way. Part of him felt challenged by her demands, and his first instinct was to defend himself. But another side of him couldn't help but be impressed by her forthright manner and honesty.

Wilson knew it was time to confide in Elsie, even if telling her the truth would end their brief, joyous relationship. 'Very well,' he said, moving to sit on the bed. 'I'll tell you everything. But I know you won't approve.' Carefully he laid down the bottle of champagne and the glasses and beckoned her to sit down next to him.

What can a lover do in this situation other than pay attention?

For the next fifteen minutes, Wilson laid bare his past and explained how his troubled upbringing and disillusionment with British government policy had ultimately led him to be recruited as a spy working against the country. The artist hid nothing, describing all the treachery he'd been involved in, and exactly how his painting skills had been utilised to send secrets inside the mattresses. Eventually he had to reveal just how closely he had worked with Green.

Elsie immediately looked disappointed. The mention of Green's name upset her, but she carried on listening intently, never once passing comment or judgment.

He looked up at her anxious face. 'I did what I did today because I wanted to be free and able to just disappear.' Taking hold of her hand, he spoke softly, 'But I don't want to do it alone. It was only when I met you again, Elsie, that I realised what I truly wanted, what I'd been missing for so long.' All Wilson's insecurities and his struggles between his desire for love and his fear of being hurt suddenly seemed to vanish. 'Every day and every year from now on, I want us to live happily together. You're good for me.'

Finally, Elsie spoke. 'You're forgetting I have Daniel.'

'No!' Wilson interrupted. 'I care very much for Daniel. I want him to be part of us. For us to live as a family. Everything can work out. And by doing what I've done today we can be that family.' He paused, realising her view could be altogether different. 'But I shall understand if you think me nothing more than a horrible traitor.'

For all her practical concerns, Elsie had made up her mind. Leaning forward, she lifted up his chin. 'What I think, is that you should open that bottle of champagne and then we can start working out how we are going to deal with this mess!'

Chapter 28

Comfortably ensconced in his office on the fourth floor, Colonel Coniston usually finished the last of his coffee by eight forty-five each morning. Then, he would thumb carefully through the daily newspapers. Not that he had any real interest in either the news or the other articles, unless they benefitted him in some way. He read the papers mainly to check that any codes that had been placed were correct, and also to see if any of the stories might offer an opportunity for agent activity.

All the secretaries knew that under no circumstances should they attempt to put through any telephone calls until well after 9 o'clock. But this particular morning, Emily Dewhirst had the unenviable task of interrupting her chief and advising him that there was a caller on the line from France – someone who had called repeatedly and insisted he speak with the colonel. Despite all her diplomacy, the senior secretary still had to endure a volley of abuse from her boss at being disturbed. 'Then I'll ask him to ring again later, sir,' she stated, satisfied that she'd tried her best.

'Did he give a name?' the colonel barked out.

'I believe it's pronounced, Monsieur Xavier Dubois,' replied Emily, attempting her best French accent.

Coniston lifted his head. It was a name he knew well. Xavier Dubois owned a storage depot which was used by the British army; but more importantly, Dubois was the contact in France who looked after the arrangement.

'You'd better put him through,' said the colonel, much to Emily's surprise.

When his phone rang, Coniston hesitated before lifting the earpiece off its cradle. Monsieur Dubois only ever rang if there was a problem. 'Yes, bonjour, Xavier,' he eventually said.

'Ah, finaleee,' started the Frenchman. 'I have been ringing you for over an hour.' His accent smoothed every word as if it was there merely to be caressed by his voice.

'Yes, sorry I had a meeting,' Coniston lied. 'Is there a problem?'

The line went momentarily quiet.

'You think it is a game, oui?'

Coniston scrunched up his brow. He didn't have a clue what Dubois was talking about. 'You know that I don't play games, Xavier. What is the problem?'

'The apartment is empty!' shouted the Frenchman.

Coniston's eyes opened wide in alarm. Apartment was the word they used when describing the mattresses.

'What, completely empty?' he cried.

'Nothing!'

The colonel was stunned. 'There must be some mistake!'

There wasn't.

~~~

For the rest of the morning, Coniston picked up the phone eagerly whenever it rang, hoping it was Monsieur Dubois with news that somehow he had got it wrong and that the mattresses were as they should be after all. Mostly though, the calls were from people checking on routine administration matters. One call, however, made the colonel sit up and take notice. He asked the secretary to confirm the name again. 'Arthur Wilson, sir,' she said.

Curious, the colonel took the call and listened to Wilson stating, 'No doubt you've had some disappointing news by now.'

Coniston remained composed. 'Go on.'

'What I've found out could be of mutual benefit.'

'I'm listening,' replied a very wary colonel.

'Not on the telephone.'

The colonel agreed and suggested a time to meet at his usual rendezvous spot.

'I'll be there,' agreed Wilson, before placing his
~~~

fingers on the cradle and disconnecting the line.

With a grin he looked over towards Elsie. 'Done!'

She returned his smile, pleased that their plan had seemingly achieved its goal.

~~~

Watching Coniston pace up and down on the pavement in front of her, Elsie took a deep breath before getting off the bench and proceeding towards her quarry. For a while she simply walked back and forth behind him, rehearsing what she was going to say. Eventually, she was comfortable enough to make her approach. 'I'm afraid Arthur Wilson won't be coming, Colonel Coniston.'

The colonel turned around in surprise. He stood looking curiously at a woman who was completely unknown to him. Who on earth was she?

Elsie gave him a pleasant smile. '... So, you've got me, instead.'

Tilting his head back slightly and peering down his nose, Coniston examined Elsie's face, trying to recall where he might have seen her before. He looked his subject up and down for what seemed like an eternity, before accepting he was unable to place her.

'And who might you be?' he finally asked, with all the arrogance that 30 years of serving in the army as an
~~~

officer had taught him.

Elsie wouldn't allow herself to be intimidated by his manner.

'It's not important who I am, colonel. Only important what I know.'

Coniston twitched his thick moustache, uneasy that he didn't have the upper hand.

'Why isn't Mr Wilson here as arranged?'

'Quite simply because he doesn't trust you, colonel,' Elsie replied and inclined her head towards the two burly intelligence men standing nearby, ready to react if given the instruction by their boss.

It was exactly as Wilson had told her would be the case.

Coniston acknowledged her astute observation and signaled with a nod for his men to stand down. 'Shall we?' he said, gesturing with his hand towards the vacant bench.

Elsie seemed to be enjoying the little game and was certainly giving a very competent performance as the spy's messenger. She sat down and pulled her heals off the ground, raising her knees to support a small purse bag. 'Mr Wilson wishes me to tell you that the apartment is empty because you've been double crossed.'

The colonel gave a pained laugh. 'That much I'd assumed, madam!' He took out a cigarette from a silver case and placed it between his lips. It immediately half disappeared underneath his large walrus moustache. 'And did Mr Wilson allude to who is double crossing me?' he enquired, with the protruding cigarette jerking about in his mouth as he spoke.

'He did indeed … Nathan Green.'

'I see.' The colonel's expression gave away nothing about what he was thinking. 'And is Nathan Green acting alone?'

'So I understand.'

'And the contents of the apartment. Does he —?'

'Yes, he has them,' interrupted Elsie.

Coniston finally lit his cigarette and inhaled deeply. 'Now a skeptic might ask why Mr Wilson would want to betray his colleague?' he said, with smoke accompanying his words.

'Let's just say he has good reason.'

The colonel started to pick off the bits of tobacco that had stuck to his tongue and bottom lip. 'How do I know it's not Wilson doing all the double crossing. He's good at that!'

Elsie again gave her pleasant smile. 'You don't. It will come down to whom you trust more.'

There was a long pause before the colonel spoke again. 'You realise I could just have those men detain you until I've spoken with Green.'

'Yes, Mr Wilson said you would say that. Which is why

he wanted me to inform you that someone is aiming a silenced revolver at you right now.'

Coniston spun round but couldn't see anyone obvious amongst the group of sightseers strolling behind them.

'Trust me, they're there,' declared Elsie, confidently.

There wasn't anybody there, but she and Wilson knew the colonel wouldn't take the chance.

'... Now, it's time for us to go our separate ways, colonel. Please signal to meet your men and start walking towards the pier.'

Coniston stroked his moustache and stood up slowly. His look at Elsie suggested deep suspicion, although he knew there was little alternative but to walk away.

Moments later, Elsie disappeared into the crowd.

Back at the hotel, she walked past the reception desk with a broad grin across her face. Everything had gone exactly as it was meant to, and, whilst she had no real desire to see Green suffer, she did hope that he would feel the consequences of her and Wilson's actions.

'Somebody looks happy,' commented the receptionist.

Elsie gave an even bigger grin, knowing it would soon be all over. She could hardly wait to join Wilson and Daniel at St Pancras Station and board the train bound for the Lake District. There, at least until the end of the war, the intention was for them to settle under the guise of a war artist, his wife and her orphaned nephew relocating following Wilson's medical discharge from the army. Longer term, their future had been very cleverly mapped out.

'Oh! Mrs Tyler,' added the receptionist, using the assumed name Elsie had given when checking in. 'Perhaps you could tell your husband that I checked the railway timetables and there is a morning train from Penrith to Glasgow this Thursday.'

Elsie's grin turned to a look of confusion. What was the woman talking about, she wondered.

A quick double check with the receptionist confirmed that Wilson had indeed asked her to get the travel information; but why, Elsie had no idea. It certainly wasn't anything they had discussed and was not, therefore, part of their plan.

The receptionist carried on chatting away, as she did with most guests who allowed her the opportunity. '… Yes, and he works all hours as well, bless him.'

Elsie, although sympathetic to the story of the telegram boy's plight, was finding the one-way conversation a little tiresome. Nothing could prepare her, however, for what she learnt next.

'Anyway. Would Mr Tyler like him to keep trying to deliver it?'

Elsie's glazed expression confirmed she hadn't really

been paying attention.

'Your husband's telegram to his sister, Mrs Tyler. Do we keep trying to deliver it or not?'

'Erm,' Elsie stumbled. She was bemused. Only three nights before they had been talking in detail about their families, and she distinctly remembered Wilson saying he was an only child. Her curiosity soon got the better of her. 'No, give it to me. I'll ensure we make alternative arrangements to get in contact with her.' Accepting the folded piece of paper given her, she opened it and began reading the message.

EVERYTHING HAS GONE AS PLANNED. NOW CAN'T WAIT FOR US ALL TO BE TOGETHER AGAIN.

It took a moment for the note to sink in. Again and again she read it, somehow hoping that she was misinterpreting things. But how could she be? The words were plain enough. All Elsie could think of was that Wilson was in a relationship with another woman. She wanted to cling to the belief that the note was meant for his sister. But if it was, then why had he lied by telling her previously that he didn't have any siblings?

'I'll take that note,' said a voice, taking her by surprise. She turned and looked with confusion at the man approaching her.

'… The note. I need to take it, Mrs Sowerby. I have to know what it says.'

Elsie's frown confirmed that she had no idea who the man was. But she didn't have long to wait for an introduction.

'My name is Brigadier Armstrong. I work in the War Office. We need to talk, ma'am.'

'I see,' replied Elsie, in a tone suggesting that she realised that whatever he wanted, it was serious.

For the next half hour the pair sat deep in conversation as though the future of the country and their own individual futures depended on what they said.

Chapter 29

St Pancras Station, London

Watching the new bride and groom further down the platform giving each other a hug, Wilson reached out and gently pulled Elsie towards him. 'One day, who knows, that might be us.'

Elsie looked up at him with what could only be described as a cautious smile. 'Yes, one day, who knows?'

Detecting an anxiety in her response, Wilson wondered what was wrong. 'Is everything all right?'

'Yes of course,' Elsie replied, with more enthusiasm, although, she could tell from his expression that he wasn't convinced. 'It's just that … well, you know me, Peter, I have to deal with what's happening in the present.'

'But you would want to marry me?'

He held his palm to her cheek. She closed her eyes as an agonising tide of uncertainty swept through her. Then the realisation of what she had agreed with Brigadier Armstrong surfaced again. Feeling Wilson's loving gaze tearing her heart apart, Elsie hoped to God she wasn't making a terrible mistake.

Needing to distract herself, she moved over to Daniel. His eyes were darting in all directions, trying to assimilate yet another adventure. 'It's all excitement isn't it?' she said, taking hold of his hand and giving it a gentle squeeze. The boy suddenly became transfixed by a plume of thick black smoke that had belched out of an engine's funnel and was travelling up towards the station's vaulted roof. Higher and higher it rose until it finally evaporated. His eyes travelled back down to the funnel, eagerly anticipating the next churn of smoke. When it came, he gave an audible 'Boom!' and spread out his arms, as if replicating an explosion. The boy's mind was somewhere on a Montana plain with the 7th Cavalry, re-enacting a battle.

'You and General Custer,' joked Elsie, carefully tapping his chin with her knuckles. 'That's our train,' she confirmed.

The boy's eyes lit up. 'What? To keep?'

Even with all her experience of Daniel's literal interpretations, Elsie still sometimes got caught out with an idiom. She smiled and explained what she'd meant, before brushing his tousled hair away from his eyes with her fingers.

The shrill sound of the guard's whistle finally indicated that boarding of the train was allowed. Daniel hurriedly grabbed at the single suitcase. Despite the audible tuts of frustration from an impatient woman who was having to wait behind him, the boy continued along the train's corridor, dragging the suitcase between his legs.

Checking each compartment carefully, Daniel came across one where there was only one man, who was reading his newspaper. He looked at his nurse for approval to enter. 'Yes, this is fine,' said Elsie and slid open the door.

Suddenly surrounded by three people, the man put down his paper and offered Wilson help in lifting the suitcase onto the luggage rack.

'No, it's all right, chaplain. I'm sure I can manage. Thanks all the same,' responded Wilson.

With steam and smoke obscuring the view out of the window, the 08:35 train departed the station. Resigned to what was happening, Elsie leant her head back on the seat, knowing that by the time they reached their first scheduled change of trains, everything would be concluded.

As they all sat in their compartment, Wilson occasionally looked up from reading his newspaper and gave Elsie a fleeting smile. She reciprocated; but beneath her smiles she was wishing fervently that everything didn't have to be this way. Checking her watch, she felt extremely tense and fidgeted on her seat, hoping that Daniel might say something – anything, just so long as it offered a distraction from her growing unease at their situation. Unfortunately, he didn't. Instead he just carried on incessantly walking his fingers back and forth on the wooden window rim, seemingly in a world of his own.

All of a sudden, something did happen to distract Elsie. To her horror, Daniel casually reached into his pocket, pulled out the now badly torn jeweller's envelope, and tipped Mary's rings into his hands. Then he started tapping them up and down on the window rim, as if they were marching soldiers.

'Daniel!' Elsie cried, unable to stifle her alarm. She reached over to take the rings and look at them properly, although she knew immediately from the envelope that they were Mary's rings, and that Daniel must have taken them. Daniel pulled away shouting, 'No!'

The army chaplain looked at Elsie and gave a smile, anticipating her chastisement of the boy. Elsie, however, was well used to having to deal with Daniel's unpredictability and calmly asked, 'Are they the rings that were on Mrs Sharpe's dressing table? And did you take them to play with?' Hearing no hostility in his nurse's voice, Daniel responded honestly with a nod of his head.

'I don't think we should let the rings get damaged. Mrs Sharpe will need them back. Why don't you let me keep them safely, and we can wrap them up later on ready to send back to her.' With that, she turned away and said nothing more, much to the surprise of the chaplain, particularly as Daniel carried on playing with the rings on the window rim. Wilson remained quiet, knowing

Elsie was firmly in control.

Moments later, the boy went and placed the rings in the palm of Elsie's hand. 'There, I've done.' He smiled, before his expression suddenly changed to a frown of puzzlement. 'Which fingers do they go on?' he enquired.

Elsie indicated her wedding finger. 'Usually they both go on this one.'

'Show me.'

'They're not my rings, Daniel. They belong to Mrs Sharpe.'

'Please!'

Knowing Daniel's tendency to keep making the same request over and over again, she decided to show him, and slid the rings onto her finger. The boy giggled and pointed. 'That one's a corporal and that one's a lieutenant.'

'Really?' said Elsie, starting to pull off the rings.

'No! Keep them on.'

Elsie was not really in the mood for any further negotiation. She decided to leave the rings on her finger for the moment, knowing it would only be a matter of time before Daniel had forgotten all about them.

Wilson looked over at her and smiled optimistically. In return, Elsie nervously fidgeted with the rings, eventually removing her hand from view.

The army chaplain, who no longer appeared to be paying any attention to the matter, took a small note book from his pocket and began scribbling.

After all that had happened to her and Daniel over the last couple of weeks, Elsie wondered whether it might simply have been better to have stayed in Sheffield and not taken Elliott's advice to stay with the Sharpes. Back home, life had been so much simpler, even boring sometimes, but at least she had been in control. Perhaps it would have been wiser to have allowed events with Daniel's mother to take their course. Dwelling on the past, however, was fruitless. She knew her focus now had to be on building a new home for them.

Constantly checking each person who walked past in the carriage corridor began to take its toll on Elsie and, before long, she had got herself into a state of panic. Trying to relax, she closed her eyes and started to breathe deeply.

The compartment door suddenly slid open, shattering her calm. Two men dressed in civilian suits walked in. The taller of these was Brigadier Armstrong, who gave a polite tilt of his hat before sitting down. He glanced at Elsie, who immediately felt impelled to look away.

The chaplain, having no reason to think there was anything strange about the men's arrival, simply carried on writing, only to be interrupted moments later by Armstrong suggesting, 'You might want to comfort the poor souls who have just been stretchered on, chaplain. Looking at them, I doubt many will make the full journey.'

Accepting that his duty these days was all about comforting the dying and seriously wounded, the chaplain rose to his feet. 'Of course, yes,' he said, packing away his notebook, 'Where are they exactly?'

'The last carriage of the train,' confirmed Armstrong, opening the door for the chaplain to exit.

Wilson was immediately suspicious, knowing that wounded soldiers were nearly always transported by hospital trains, but he pretended to carry on reading his newspaper.

Elsie sat rigid in anticipation that Armstrong and his colleague would soon be making their move. Meanwhile, Daniel continued staring out of the window, totally ignoring the fact that two newcomers had arrived and sat down beside him. Then, out of the blue, the boy proudly announced, 'I fought in the battle of Little Bighorn.'

For a brief moment, the comment eased the tension that had filled the small compartment.

'Did you now?' acknowledged Armstrong, willing to humour the boy.

'Yes, and —'

Interrupting Daniel, Wilson stood up, but found his way to the door was discretely blocked by the shorter man, whose raincoat was folded over his arm, disguising a revolver. The artist's fear that the men were intelligence agents was quickly realised. He wasn't prepared though, for what happened next, and could only look on in utter amazement when Armstrong turned to Elsie and said, 'Well, thank you very much, Mrs Sowerby. I think you can safely leave us to deal with Mr Wilson.'

The brigadier slid open the door for her and Daniel to leave.

'What!' cried Wilson, in disbelief.

Overcome by the part she was playing, Elsie could hardly bring herself to look at her lover. But eventually she lifted her eyes to meet his. 'I'm sorry, Peter … I'm so, so sorry,' she murmured, in a tearful voice.

'Elsie, why?' The bewildered Wilson opened his hands wide.

'This telegram to your "sister"!' she replied, holding up the piece of paper the hotel receptionist had given her.

'No!' protested Wilson. 'You've misunderstood. I can explain.'

Elsie diverted her eyes from his distressed face. 'I realise now that I could never truly trust you, Peter.'

Wilson was bursting with frustration. 'Elsie, please!'

Once more looking apologetic, she continued, 'I have to do the right thing for the country.'

So far Daniel had been impassive, but now he was beginning to get agitated. Although he could listen intently to a conversation or argument between two people and understand the words, he struggled to comprehend what was actually happening. Seeing sad and shocked faces made him uneasy. Elsie knew she had to re-assure him that everything was all right as she moved towards the door. 'Come, Daniel,' she said, 'We have to move compartments now.'

'Yes, all right,' he accepted, and held out his hand for Wilson to guide him.

'No, just you and me for now,' she interjected, before placing her hands at the side of his eyes to form blinkers. Daniel gave her his attention and listened as she carefully explained, 'Peter can't come with us right now. He has to stay and speak with these gentlemen. We'll see him later.'

Regret at having to lie to Daniel ripped through her, especially as she gave a promise, which she knew would not be fulfilled.

Finally, knowing that this was the only course of action she could have taken, Elsie composed herself and stood up tall. Determinedly holding Daniel's hand and leading him through the door, she stopped and gave the devastated Wilson one last glance. 'I pray that God will watch over you, Peter.'

At the next stop, she watched as Wilson was escorted off the train, knowing that he would already have been told he was to be returned to London and charged with treason. Everything had happened just as Brigadier Armstrong said it would.

Her reflection in the window clearly showed the tears rolling down her cheek. Anxiety about the fate of the man being dragged away gripped her heart. With her thumb, she rolled the rings round on her finger before carefully pulling them off and placing them in her purse.

Quite where the kindly chaplain had got to, Elsie didn't even wonder.

Chapter 30

Clerical superintendant Cybil Kelsett fell back in her chair, stunned at what Coniston was telling her. Like him, she couldn't quite believe the mattresses were empty. 'How could that have happened?' she argued. 'Everything was organised to the last detail by me.' Hearing that Nathan Green was responsible for the situation shocked her even more. Whilst she knew the doctor was clever and deceitful, she would never have imagined that he would turn and bite the hand of those who, effectively, fed him. The colonel quickly reminded her that, when the opportunity arose, Green would stop at nothing to benefit himself.

Miss Kelsett looked on as Coniston started to scribble furiously on his pad. With a forceful stroke of his pen to underline his signature, he ripped off the sheet and handed it over to her. 'There are my instructions. All available personnel to look for Green. I want no stone left unturned to find him.'

With her own interests very much at stake, Kelsett ensured that every suitable member of staff was drafted into the search.

Green had anticipated that Wilson would betray him to the British intelligence service, and this made going home too risky. With the safe house on Ivy Street once again empty, he decided he would be better off there. What he couldn't have foreseen was that his colleague would go direct to Coniston; but then Green had no idea that weeks earlier a disillusioned and worried Wilson had approached the colonel, wanting to hedge his bets for the future and offer himself as a double agent.

This meant that, although the doctor was carefully watching his back, he was actually looking out for the wrong people.

After a heavy dose of painkillers and a sound night's sleep, Green woke to find he felt remarkably well, given what he had been through. Whilst he could still feel some pain at the back of his head, he no longer had any symptoms of concussion. All things considered, he had been extremely lucky to come out of his experience with only minimal injuries.

Green's most acute problem now was the pressure of time. With Maude waiting in Peterborough, his priority was how he could get Mary to accompany him there. Any business with Wilson would, for the moment, have to remain unfinished. He pondered hard on what might be the most convincing reason for her to board the train with him, but knew that whatever reason he chose, it had to include either Tom or baby Lucinda. Experience had long ago taught him that people would do almost anything when their family was under threat.

In the end, he decided to go for the easiest option first – Tom. If that didn't work, then he would fall back on a more drastic plan. Wandering around the house, Green rehearsed his story, anticipating any questions or objections Mary might raise. It really ought to be quite simple, he thought, and began to make his preparations by bathing and shaving.

Arriving at the Sharpes' house, Green stopped short as he saw Mary outside, watering a hanging basket of flowers. He studied her beauty once more and for a brief moment doubted whether he had made the right decision; but as in any situation that posed a dilemma for him, he quickly found that a voice inside his head took control. 'Remember Maude,' it said. 'Poor, poor Maude.'

Green shuddered and began to focus once again.

'Oh hello, Mr Green,' said Mary. 'I thought it looked like you.'

Like an actor in a play watching the curtain rise before him, Green was suddenly thrust in front of his audience. Today, he knew, he had to deliver the most convincing performance of his life.

'Were you coming to see me?' asked Mary.

'Yes, I was, as a matter of fact.' He allowed his cheerful expression to slowly fade into one of unease and sadness.

Mary immediately picked up on his change of countenance. 'It's to do with Tom, isn't it?'

Green nodded.

'Oh no.' Mary took a deep breath. 'Please, you'd better come in, Mr Green.'

Standing in the hallway, Green began to create a sense of urgency. 'I'll have to be brief, Mrs Sharpe, if I'm to catch the train to see Tom.'

Not surprisingly, Mary took the bait straight away. 'Train to see Tom. What do you mean?'

Green gave an exasperated sigh. 'I knew nobody would have told you. This is exactly why I needed to come.' After a sympathetic shrug of his shoulders, he went on to explain that intelligence officers had now decided to charge Tom and, because of the nature of the accusations, they were transferring him to military barracks in Peterborough, ahead of a court hearing.

Nobody could accuse Green of not giving a compelling performance. He started looking at his watch anxiously. 'I really must go to catch the train, Mrs Sharpe. I'll let you know as soon as I have any more news.'

He was half out of the door when she called out, 'Wait! Please.' She put her hand to her head, flustered, just as he intended her to be. 'I … er … I …,' she stuttered. 'I think I should come with you, Mr Green.'

He gave a worried look. 'But what about your baby?'

'Well … I'll ….' Mary started thinking, desperately, until eventually, she came up with a solution. 'I'll ask our neighbour, Mrs Hughes, if she'll take Lucinda until I get back. Lucinda's very used to her.'

Green paused and puffed out his cheeks for dramatic effect. 'If you're sure, then yes.' He checked his watch again. 'But we'll have to be quick.'

Within ten minutes, Mrs Hughes had been commandeered for babysitting duty and Mary was accompanying Green towards Finsbury Park Station.

Not all things were destined to go according to the doctor's plan however. As their tube pulled into Kings Cross, Green was recognised by one of Coniston's intelligence team, who hastily made a telephone call to his boss.

~~~

Aboard the 11:15 train bound for Peterborough

After a delay of 30 minutes, the train finally began to roll forward. The guard, thoroughly fed up with incurring the wrath of disgruntled passengers, gave an audible sigh,
~~~

relieved that he would no longer need to keep placating people.

Nobody was more relieved than Green that the locomotive was on the move. The doctor looked over to Mary opposite him and gave her his well-practised, reassuring smile. 'Shouldn't be long now before we're there.'

Mary wasn't really paying much attention, but did respond with a delicate smile of acknowledgement, before returning to her concerns for Tom. Although she was strong and practical, the anxiety of the situation was now beginning to show on Mary's face.

Green began constantly checking his watch, going over his timings. It really wasn't necessary, as his plan was relatively straightforward, but this was a habit the doctor had when apprehensive. Once again he went over the calculation in his head. He had to get it just right, otherwise it could be disastrous. Too much solution would simply make her unconscious. Too little and she would still be able to speak properly, as well as being able to struggle or fight back. It all had to look as though Mary had suddenly become ill, but not to the extent that an ambulance needed calling.

Further down the train, in the corridor of a goods carriage, was the reason for the delay in departure: Colonel Coniston, who had insisted the train be held back until he got to the station. Trying to stand upright as the wagon swayed from side to side on the crossover track, he watched his agent gesturing towards where Green was located.

'Excellent!' said the colonel, before going back into the goods compartment itself. Now it was simply a case of waiting until Green passed the door and dragging him inside at gunpoint. Checking his revolver, Coniston anticipated the conversation would be a brief one.

The trouble was, simply relying on Green getting up for a toilet break was folly. The colonel needed to think how else he could get the doctor to walk down the corridor that passed along the side of the goods carriage. Of course, he could have had his men go in and drag Green out of his compartment; but he really had no desire to create a scene which would cause a lot of unwanted attention. It was far preferable to come up with a reason that would force the doctor to leave his compartment. In the end, the colonel decided on something quite straightforward and had an agent fetch the guard to assist.

'... So, you understand exactly what to do?' the colonel asked.

'Er, yes, I think so,' replied the guard, 'Just one question, though. What if there is another doctor in one of the compartments before his. What do I do then?'

The colonel rolled his eyes in despair, although he realized the guard's question was a good one.

'Just bring him to me and I'll deal with it,' insisted the colonel.

The guard, appearing to understand everything, pulled down his waistcoat and pushed back his shoulders, feeling like an indispensible part of some highly important war office business.

In the compartment, Mary was trying to distract herself from worrying by attempting to read the headlines of a newspaper being read by the man opposite her; although, in her anxious state, she would have found it impossible to recall any of the text if asked. Green was sitting deep in thought, once again playing out his plan, step by step, in his mind: trick her into corridor - check gauze – eight paces – pull emergency chord – catch hold – gauze over face – count …. A voice calling out in the distance broke his concentration. Everyone strained to hear until, eventually, the words of the guard became louder and clearer. 'Is there a doctor on the train? … Is there a doctor on the train?'

Green cursed, knowing he wouldn't be able to deny the fact when the guard came into their compartment. Inevitably, the door slid open.

'Yes, I'm a doctor,' Green reluctantly acknowledged in response to the guard's question.

'Sir, we have a gentleman further down the train who has collapsed unconscious. Would you be good enough to assist?'

'Well —' began Green, desperately wondering whether there was any way he might be able to get out of going.

'Oh please, you must go, Mr Green,' Mary interrupted.

'Of course,' answered the doctor and picked up his small medicine bag. 'Lead the way please, guard.'

Normally, Green was acutely aware of his surroundings. As an agent, he had honed his skills in detecting potential danger. Today, however, his preoccupation with Mary and a sense of all he needed to achieve combined to make him less wary. He simply followed the guard without question. That is until he heard the cocking of a gun behind him. Slowly coming to a halt, he turned round to see Colonel Coniston aiming a revolver directly at him.

'Hello, Nathan,' declared the colonel with a sinister stare. 'Sorry about the gun – only way we can get fare dodgers to pay, you see.'

Green gave a forced half smile at the colonel's attempted humour and took a look into the goods compartment into which he was being directed. Letting out an exasperated sigh, he asked, 'Am I allowed to ask what all this stupidity is about?'

The colonel only responded with another flick of his gun towards the door.

In minimal light, and surrounded by large boxes stacked four high, Green asked again. 'What is this all about, colonel?'

'I have to hand it to you, Nathan, your skill as an actor has always impressed me.'

Green frowned.

'… Let's make things simple, shall we? You either tell me where the contents of the mattresses have gone – or I put a bullet straight through your head!'

There was no doubting the colonel meant what he said. He was as ruthless as anyone Green had ever encountered in the secret service. The realisation that he was being set up began to hit him. And he was beginning to suspect who was behind it.

'Look colonel, whatever you've been told, it's a lie. I don't know anything about the contents of the mattresses going missing,' pleaded Green, holding up his hands.

Coniston wasn't a man of great sympathy. 'Save it for the pearly gates. I'm sure St. Peter will listen.'

'It's Wilson, isn't it?' asked Green. 'He's made an approach to you with some complete fabrication implicating me.' He laughed. 'You've been cleverly deceived, colonel.'

The colonel stood unfazed. Clenching his teeth, he transformed his expression into a menacing glare and demanded to know, 'Where are the contents?'

'I think we both now know the only person who has the answer to that is Arthur Wilson.'

Gradually, the colonel was arriving at the conclusion

that Green was actually telling the truth.

Green could sense as much. 'So, now what?'

After taking a moment to reflect, the colonel coldly redirected his revolver to Green's heart and squeezed the trigger three times, watching the doctor jerk as each silenced shot was absorbed by his body.

Briefly, Green's eyes opened wide in shock, before rolling upwards. Finally, he slumped down in a heap.

'Sorry ol' boy,' muttered the colonel. 'It's now all about who's of further use to me.'

As the train began to pull into Peterborough, Mary assumed Green must still be dealing with the sick patient somewhere on board. When the engine finally came to a halt, she waited patiently for him to arrive back. But, as the train emptied and there then appeared to be little activity, she decided she would go in search of the doctor. Seeing a porter loading some sacks, she asked, 'Do you know which carriage has the poorly man?'

'Poorly man, miss?'

'Yes, there's a sick man on the train who needed assistance. My doctor friend went —'

The porter interrupted her with the flat statement that, 'There's no passengers left on the train.'

Confused, Mary continued walking down the corridor, checking each compartment. But there was no-one. Stepping out of a carriage onto the platform, she enquired of another porter. 'Excuse me, sir, but has a sick man, accompanied by a doctor, been brought this way.'

'Not to my knowledge, miss.'

Mary stood still, baffled as to what was going on. Catching the porter's attention again, she enquired. 'How far are the military barracks?'

Her question was met with a look of confusion. 'Ain't no military barracks in Peterborough, as I'm aware of,' replied the porter.

Unable to make sense of what was happening, Mary sighed with frustration. It all seemed so odd. Little could she have imagined just how lucky she had been. Twenty minutes later, the guard was blowing his whistle for the train's departure back to London. Unsure what to do for the best, Mary decided to follow her instinct and take the return journey.

On board, a concerned and anxious Mary slid open a compartment door and entered. Inside sat a man clutching a book in his hand. Mary sat down and fanned her face in the rising heat. He gave a jolly smile and ran a finger along the inside of his dog collar. 'Yes, warm isn't it?' said the army chaplain.

Chapter 31

Aboard the 1:40 train bound for St Pancras, London.

These days, when travelling, indeed whenever she went out, Emily was always looking about her, worrying whether she would be disposed of, like Dakin. The young secretary desperately wished she had never found out the truth. In the intelligence game, a combination of unquenchable curiosity, access to information, and the ability to process that information could be a recipe for disaster. And, if there was one thing that Emily had learnt in her time at Adelphi Court, it was that people who knew too much invariably disappeared, seemingly without trace. Anxiously, she twisted her wedding ring round on her finger, wishing her new husband was with her. He always helped her keep things in perspective.

Emily started to recall the day she had discovered what had happened. Had she not wanted to catch up on a filing backlog, she wouldn't have been in the filing room, located across from Cybil Kelsett's office, in her lunch break. It was rare for her superintendant to leave her door open; but since, on this occasion, she had, Emily tried hard not to pay attention to the conversation she could hear between her boss and Colonel Coniston. The colonel was ranting about Dakin, and it wasn't long before his words caught the young secretary's interest. As the discussion continued, she found herself listening even more intently. She moved ever closer towards Kelsett's door.

The conversation quickly became heated.

'I distinctly said drowning. A bludgeoned body attracts all sorts of unwanted attention,' snapped the colonel.

'I know. I'm sorry. It didn't exactly go according to plan,' Kelsett explained.

He gave a guffaw. 'No, nothing ever bloody well does.'

'I think they just underestimated his strength.'

The colonel sighed before telling Kelsett, 'We need this to be reported in the press as a suicide: drowning due to depression, pressure of his personal circumstances, that sort of thing.'

'Of course.'

'And, who have we got who can get at the coroner's report? It may need altering.'

What Emily wasn't expecting was that Coniston would grab the door and fling it shut. His actions made her jump and she gasped loudly in shock. The pile of paperwork in her arms fell to the floor.

Slowly the door reopened and the colonel stood

looking at her. 'Hello, Miss Dewhirst,' he said calmly. 'And how long have you been out here?'

'Oh, only a second, sir,' replied Emily, thinking quickly. 'I was taking these papers to the filing room when you slammed the door and frightened me half to death.'

She remembered the look on Coniston's face. He hadn't been totally convinced.

Allowing her thoughts to return to the present, Emily sat in the compartment becoming more and more nervous of the soldier seated by the window with his chin resting on his hand. Why did he keep looking at her, she couldn't help wondering. Was this the time? Was he the person whom the colonel had sent to kill her? Her increasing panic subsided slightly as the soldier moved his hand, revealing a dog collar and an obvious rank as an army chaplain. For a brief moment, she began to feel safe. That is until she saw someone's shadow fall slowly across the corridor.

With her eyes squeezed tightly together, she waited, anticipating the door was going to slide open at any moment.

Indeed, it did.

Emily was so gripped by her anxiety that she didn't at first hear the new arrival's voice. Only after the ticket attendant repeated his words assertively did her thoughts return to reality. Nervously, she fumbled in her purse for her ticket.

When the chaplain could see that Emily's obvious agitation was not abating, he felt compelled to mention his concern. 'Please excuse me, miss, but ever since entering the compartment, I couldn't help noticing the worried look on your face. Is everything alright?'

~~~

Feeling a hand clasped firmly over her mouth, Emily struggled with all her might to free herself, but her attacker's grip was strong and she was quickly pulled off balance. In the darkness she fell. For a moment, as she went down, she felt warm breath on her ear; but the person said nothing.

The train thundered out of the tunnel, allowing daylight to fill the corridor. Slowly, the hand was released from over her mouth, finally allowing Emily to turn enough to see a face. Her suspicion as to her attacker was confirmed.

'Hello Emily!' said the familiar voice.

'Miss Kelsett! Emily cried, 'Please! Please! Don't kill me. I'll do whatever you like, just don't —'

Kelsett interrupted, her tone a disturbing mix of reassurance and unyielding severity. 'Emily, my dear, if only it worked like that, life would be so much easier. But
~~~

the rules are very simple. You know that.'

'The other day in the office, I swear I didn't hear anything,' insisted Emily, now facing a revolver.

The sickly smile on Kelsett's face indicated to Emily that her continued pleading would be to no avail.

'Your rings, watch and pendant,' Kelsett demanded, holding out her hand.

'But why?'

'Oh come now, Emily,' Kelsett scoffed.

Of course Emily knew exactly why she was being required to hand over her jewellery. She'd worked in the service long enough to know that personal items were always taken from captives who were killed, in order to make it harder to identify their bodies. Equally disturbing were the rumours she'd heard of Kelsett and Coniston taking personal items and selling them for personal gain.

With reluctance Emily untied her watch and handed it over, all the while desperately thinking how she might be able to escape. The possibility, however, seemed more and more unlikely as she looked into the barrel of Kelsett's revolver.

'It was my mother's,' cried Emily, finally lifting the pendant from around her neck.

Kelsett showed no hint of emotion as she took it. Instead, she merely gestured with the gun towards the rings.

'No, not my rings! I won't let you have them.'

'Perhaps, you need some encouragement?' Kelsett cooly replied and redirected her aim towards Emily's knees.

'All right! All right!'

Emily pulled off her engagement and wedding rings and sorrowfully moved to drop them into Kelsett's open palm. Sorrow turned to shock when Kelsett suddenly turned over her hand and spread out her fingers. 'Put them on my finger.'

It was the final humiliation for Emily, having to see her rings on another woman's finger; but she had no option but to do as she was told.

'Very nice,' said Kelsett, inspecting the rings. Seeing Emily's reaction, she taunted the young woman further, holding out her hand and purring, 'Yes, very nice indeed.'

Just as Emily was resigning herself to her fate, the train entered another tunnel, plunging the carriage into darkness once more. Knowing she wouldn't get a better chance of escape, she reached out and grabbed Kelsett's hand. At that moment the revolver went off. Emily felt a sharp pain in her leg and was convinced the bullet had entered at the front and exited at the back. In reality the shot had merely grazed her leg, but her survival instinct immediately took over and she wrestled her attacker for the revolver. Eventually, she was able to grip enough of Kelsett's arm to keep banging it against the carriage wall. She was rewarded by hearing the sound of the gun falling to the ground. Desperately, she kicked all around, before at last connecting with the gun and sending it flying away.

Kelsett's strength quickly helped her gain control again and meant she was once more able to clasp a hand around Emily's face. Immediately, the secretary's hands thrashed about against the side of the carriage, trying to grab hold of anything firm enough to prevent her from being dragged to the ground. Bumping around, Kelsett felt a door handle suddenly thud into her back. Shrieking with pain, she momentarily loosened her vice-like grip.

Emily sank her teeth deep into the soft flesh between Kelsett's forefinger and thumb. Again, Kelsett howled in agony. 'Cow!' she cried, and lashed out with a clenched fist. Never before had Emily experienced a punch in the face. Wincing, she attempted another bite, only to feel another punch, this time to the side of her stomach.

On the verge of exhaustion, Emily made one last attempt to grasp something, eventually catching hold of the door handle and managing to turn it.

The sudden opening of the door sent a rush of air and a volley of steam and smoke cascading through the carriage. Back and forth the door clattered, between the side of the train and the blackened, damp stone of the tunnel wall.

The sound was deafening.

As the struggle between the pair continued, they

desperately tried to cling onto something in the carriage, but with horror felt themselves being pulled towards the opening. Kelsett used all her strength to try and heave the door shut; but the pressure was far too powerful. Again and again the door rebounded off the wall until, with one almighty crash, it came right off its hinges and fell away, breaking into pieces.

Speeding out of the tunnel, the carriage was again bathed in daylight. Unfortunately, with the light came a sharp back draft of air, which instantly propelled Emily straight through the opening like some tossed rag doll.

Kelsett stumbled and found herself lying half in and half out of the opening. She caught only a glimpse of the track flying by below her before her long, flowing dress was sucked out and became enmeshed in the turning wheels below, instantly dragging her down. Her scream faded almost straight away. What was left of her body was now deposited on the couplings.

With a loud sound of its whistle, the train made its final descent into St Pancras Station.

Chapter 32

After several days in a dank cell, with no daylight at all, Tom squinted in the sunlight, trying to adjust to the overwhelming brightness. Released from custody at last, he stood for a moment outside the police station and lent back, taking the deepest breath of fresh air possible. 'Ahh, yes!' he cried, swinging his arms around in a circular motion before finally doing two squats, much to the bewilderment of passers-by, who gave him the strangest of looks.

Tom knew the area well enough to be aware of which route would take him to the tube station. He set off walking, utterly relieved that he was free. All he wanted to do now was to get home and see Mary and baby Lucinda. If being locked up in a cell, surrounded by the drunks and strays of society, had taught him anything, it was to appreciate freedom and to thank the lord for having the love of a family and friends. He gave a thought to some of the unfortunate people he'd met. As a professor of surgery, he was used to controlling the outcomes of life; but his experience over the last few days had shown him how many members of the police, who held that same power, merely abused it.

As Tom approached the tube station, it suddenly occurred to him that he might not have any coins to pay for the fare home. Although he remembered having some in his pocket when he was charged and stripped of his clothing, he hadn't thought to check the cash was still there when he was given back his belongings. Plunging his hands into his pockets, he found a reassuring small pile of copper and silver in one of them.

Immensely relieved to be finally arriving at St Pancras Station, Tom made his way across the platform, his mind pre-occupied with the thought that he would soon be able to take a long hard soak in the bathtub. Although he was initially oblivious of the crowd gathering around the train that had just pulled in, the gasps and chatter eventually caught his attention. A woman's horrified look and accompanying scream made him turn and want to investigate.

~~~

Doctor Goddard relaxed his grip on Tom as he finally stopped struggling. 'Tom, what do you mean, it's Mary?' shouted the alarmed coroner's assistant.

Still weeping, Tom again picked up the limp hand
~~~

hanging from the body. Barely able to speak from emotion, he touched the rings. 'These …' He swallowed, trying to get rid of the lump forming in his throat. Eventually, he managed to continue. 'These rings. They're Mary's!'

Goddard gave a nervous laugh. 'They could just be very similar ones, Tom.'

'I know they're Mary's,' Tom insisted.

'No! I'm sure not.'

The doctor was trying his best to remain optimistic. He looked towards the police constable, who was still partially holding Tom, and gestured to him to let go.

Becoming a little more composed, Tom wiped away his tears. 'The only way we'll know is by checking for her scar, William.'

'What's is all this about a scar?'

Tom explained how Mary had undergone a cesarean section after her accident. He stifled a sob and dropped his head slightly. 'I'll know when I see the scar.'

Goddard let out a sigh. 'Oh come now, Tom. Even if she does have a scar, that doesn't necessarily mean it is Mary. Lots of women in London have had a section.'

Tom lifted his head and fixed his stare straight at the doctor. 'I helped perform the surgery, William, and then stood over my wife every day for a week wondering whether she would make it. Believe me, I'll know if it's her scar or not!'

'Very well,' replied Goddard. 'Let's check.' He asked the constable to fetch a sheet or blanket that could be held up to shield them from view, not that the crowd would see much. Bystanders had now been moved some way back from the incident. Still, it was a practice that Goddard insisted on when removing garments at a scene. With some apprehension, he began to pick at the items of clothing which Tom had already ripped away, until the corset was fully exposed. Turning over the body, he started to untie the lacing.

Holding his breath, Tom spread his hand across his chin and rubbed anxiously at his stubble. Finally, as the body was turned back, he slumped down on his knees, his hand moving over his eyes to staunch the tears. Only this time, they were tears of joy. He stared down at the unblemished skin of the woman's stomach and allowed himself to breathe once more.

Despite all the drama that was unfolding on Platform 3, departures and arrivals were continuing in the rest of the station. Not the least of these was a train returning from Peterborough, which was now arriving on Platform 4 with Mary on board. Still bemused as to where Green had disappeared to, Mary decided she would make a brief enquiry at the station manager's office, thinking it might be possible that the sick patient and Green had been brought back by another train or route. Unsurprisingly, her enquiry turned up nothing. Yet again she was told that no sick person had been transported through the station that day. Not for the first time, Mary suspected there might be something devious at play.

Making her way towards the underground, she came up against the crowd of people cordoned off from what was clearly some kind of incident. Pushing her way through the mass of bodies, she pulled up at the insistence of a police constable who was holding his arm out to stop anyone moving forward.

Mary watched as a blanket-covered stretcher was brought up from the platform to a waiting ambulance. Seeing the person who was accompanying the stretcher made her gasp in shock. 'Tom!' she cried and broke through the cordon. Not even a fence of barbed wire would have stopped her getting to her husband. She flung herself at Tom and wrapped her arms around him. 'Oh, dear lord, you're safe,' she said, laying her head against his chest.

Tom was as shocked as Mary, if not more so. He couldn't believe it: only minutes earlier he had been preparing himself to accept that his wife was dead; and now here she was, clinging on to him.

'Tom, I thought you were —'

'And I thought you were ... Good god, it is you!' Tom stood trying to assimilate it all. Then he took her head in his hands and started to kiss her brow repeatedly, before finally drawing her into a loving embrace and giving her a tender kiss on the lips.

Mary was taken aback by her husband's sudden outpouring of emotion. Whilst Tom was always affectionate, she'd never witnessed anything quite as like this, particularly when they were in public. 'I don't know exactly where you've been, dear, but if this is what happens when you come back, you have my full permission to go there again,' she joked, extricating herself from his grip.

He pulled her back and just stared at her. 'Oh Mary!' Once more, he hugged her tightly.

Beginning to feel slightly embarrassed, Mary smiled at the sea of faces now peering at her and Tom. She tapped her husband to get him to release his hold; but it was too late to stop the spontaneous round of applause. Both began to laugh, and cuddled each other again.

Walking towards the office where Goddard had taken the body, Tom started to explain what had happened; but first he held up and studied her left hand. 'Mary, where are your wedding rings?'

She looked at her undressed third finger. 'Oh, they're at home. Why?'

Tom answered her by asking another question, 'They're definitely at home?'

'Well, yes.' His query though, made her begin to doubt

herself. 'They should be on the dressing table, still in the jewellery company's envelope so they can go back for re-sizing. Remember? I told you, Mrs Sowerby collected them for me, but when I tried them they were too big.'

'And nobody has moved them?'

'Well, no I don't think so. Although, if I'm honest, I'll admit I haven't checked. Why? Tom, what on earth is wrong?

'It's a long, long story, Mary.'

Of course, the rings had gone missing from the dressing table. As Elsie Sowerby found out Daniel had simply taken them. Quite what was going through the boy's mind at the time was impossible to say. Sometimes, Daniel did things for no apparent reason. However, his nurse was sure of one thing: Daniel taking the rings would have been influenced in some way by his fixation with the 7th Cavalry.

Assuming that the rings must have somehow been stolen from the house and quickly sold on, Tom explained the situation to Doctor Goddard. Two days later, he and Mary visited the coroner's office and were presented with the rings. Mary didn't need to have them checked for authenticity: she instinctively knew they weren't hers and were fakes. Turning to Goddard, she gave him back the rings. 'I doubt we'll ever know why the poor woman was wearing them. But whatever the reason, I think they ought to rest in peace with her.'

Chapter 33

Elsie stared out of the parlour window, her expressionless face watching the myriads of grey clouds roll down over the fells towards the lake in the distance. At times they were so low it seemed they were almost dancing across the water. The views from her rented cottage in Cumbria could only be described as stunning, yet she never felt any real affinity with the place. Despite all its coziness, to her it was just a temporary base before moving on. Daniel, on the other hand, had taken to the small village dwelling and appeared quite happy, always playing with his soldiers on a rug in front of the roaring fire. Only once had he asked about Peter's whereabouts, but then willingly accepted his nurse's explanation that he had to stay away on business for a while.

By the side of her armchair, lying on a small circular table with a well-worn green leather top, was a folded newspaper with just a single column headline showing. It read: *'Traitors get justice'*. The title indicated the enormity of the treason involved; but the heavily censored article gave only the briefest details of a guilty verdict on three unnamed men who had been tried for espionage in a closed courtroom. This was how little the public would learn of the truth: of the many top secrets that had been sent to the enemy; of the scale of the spy ring which had infiltrated the British establishment.

Elsie read only the openng paragraph before gently placing the paper back on the table and moving towards the window:

Yesterday at the Old Bailey, an espionage trial held in closed session reached a conclusion, and reporting restrictions were lifted in part. Guilty verdicts were passed on three defendants. The honourable Mr Justice Kilner Kt. handed down the maximum sentence of death in all cases ...

The unnamed people referred to were, in fact, Colonel Edward Coniston, Major Richard Raven and Arthur Wilson. Many more people would be charged over the coming months for aiding and abetting their espionage. However, the bigger prize being sought was the identification of a group of members of the most privileged classes, particularly a government minister, who were involved in a massive forgery which had been running alongside the sending of secrets in mattresses. 'The arrangement', as it was called, involved the illegal printing of high-quality French bank notes in a London warehouse. Over two years of printing, it was estimated that over 18 million francs had been produced and sent to France in scores of mattresses. All of this money had been put into the system and circulated.

The discovery of the fraud was in part a direct result of Wilson's knowledge and information, which Elsie Sowerby had passed on to Brigadier Armstrong.

Once the scandal had finally run its course, Elsie made two telephone calls – the first to a storage company in London, requesting the delivery of mattresses they were holding for her; the second to an international removals company to discuss and organise a move to France.

~~~

Sheffield, 1919

Ann bent down to scoop up the mail from the mat in the hallway. As was normal, the letters for her husband numbered upwards of half a dozen. Elliott, adjusting his tie in the mirror, made his usual enquiry: 'Anything for me, dear?'

Flicking through the pile, Ann decided to tease him. 'Well, that must be a first. Not one for you, Robert.' She smiled mischievously and took the letters into the dining room. Elliott's look of disappointment was a picture.
~~~

'Really? None for me?' he asked, following his wife.

Ann held the letters over her shoulder for him. 'Don't panic, I was only joking.' She shook her head in amusement as they sat down at the table, where she watched Elliott eagerly opening his envelopes. 'I wouldn't mind if there was ever anything interesting in them.'

'They're all interesting,' declared Elliott.

'No they're not,' she laughed, picking up a letter and reading it, 'Proposed amendment to Clause (f) Section 2 of the … Oh, I'm sure this will be scintillating reading!'

Elliott snatched back the letter. 'Well they're interesting to me.'

By now their sons, Henry and Cecil had joined them at the table.

Working his way through his pile of envelopes, Elliott was intrigued by one which was addressed in the most beautiful handwriting. Studying it further, he noticed it had a French stamp and postmark. 'Umm, one here from France.' Handing it to Henry, he said with a deadpan expression, 'There you go, son. You're good at French. You can read it to me.'

Henry looked up, wearing a frown. 'Father, just because it's from France doesn't mean it's written in French.'

'Well, silly me,' teased Elliott.

Ann intervened to prevent any cross words. 'I think father was only joking, Henry.'

The sulking young man gave a shrug and returned to eating his toast.

Sipping his tea, Elliott started to read Elsie Sowerby's letter which, to be sure of concealing her current location, she'd posted during a trip to Paris. No sooner had he started reading than he was on the edge of his seat in his eagerness to pursue her story.

My Dear Mr Elliott,

I sincerely hope that once you've read my letter, you will burn it. I feel impelled to write, because I have always been anxious to explain things to you and your wife. But only now, a full year after the war has ended, do I feel it safe to do so.

Where shall I begin? I can only express my heartfelt apologies for what you must all consider my strange behaviour and terrible rudeness, particulary towards Mr and Mrs Sharpe, to whom I intend writing separately. The rudeness, however, was merely the consequence of a very complicated situation which I shall now tell you all about ...

Elliott sat reading Elsie's story with his mouth open in amazement. Occasionally, his eyebrows lifted at the sheer unlikeliness of it all. In his job, he was used to dealing with deceit; but the scale of this example truly staggered him. With each new paragraph, he felt his anger rising and began berating himself for what Elsie had endured. Why hadn't he followed his instinct about Green and investigated him, he kept asking himself. Eventually, he read about what Elsie described as her betrayal of Wilson, and about the money in the mattresses, which now funded her new life. His heart sank.

… But please, Mr Elliott, don't make your final judgement of me until you have finished my letter …

As he carried on reading, Elliott was at least heartened to learn of Daniel's happiness in his surroundings, and his progress.

… And so we've discovered our happiness here in France. For obvious reasons, I cannot tell you where I am in the country, but believe me when I tell you we live in the most heavenly place, which both Daniel and I have grown to love. People here are poor, but they have a lifestyle I can only envy. They work so hard on their land, from which many of the men have gone forever. Yet when they have a celebration, there is no greater pleasure than to see how much they love their life and their village. Regrettably, I am still struggling to master the language. However, Daniel fares much, much better than me. You really should see him, Mr Elliott, and how he has progressed. He

Elsie had allowed her thoughts to drift back to the day everything had begun, with a conversation with Madame Thierry at the post office.

'Oui, it is true, Madame. The van brings your friend here as we speak,' declared the post mistress in her pidgin English.

What she was alluding to was a trip her husband

was taking in his taxi to pick up a man from the railway station at the nearest town and bring him to the village.

Elsie suddenly became flustered.

'Here, here,' shouted Madame Thierry, excitedly holding up a small, ancient mirror. 'Ah oui, vous êtes belle, très belle! Go now!'

Elsie straightened her dress and patted her hair one last time before running out into the small square. Beside herself with anticipation, she paced up and down in a small patch of shade outside the auberge. Eventually, she heard a horn sounding as a car bounced its way down the winding, cobbled road. She slipped out into the brilliant sunshine and waited on the bleached sandstone pavement.

Out of a haze of sunlight, he suddenly appeared, walking towards her, holding his jacket over his shoulder with one hand and carrying a battered cream suitcase with the other. His hair, which she had always seen slicked back with oil, had now dried out and hung down his forehead in ringlets. 'Hello, Elsie,' he said, his parched voice cracking with emotion.

Elsie's face was wreathed in smiles. He was finally here, the reason for all her struggles, the person she truly wanted to share the rest of her life with and was determined never to let slip away.

With tear-filled eyes she fell into his arms. 'Oh, Peter, thank god you're here.'

He pulled up her head and gently kissed her lips. Smiling, he whispered 'Henry, remember, Henry.'

Brigadier Armstrong had kept the promise he had given Elsie on the day he had revealed himself as the 'sister' to whom Peter was sending a telegram.

… So you see, Mr Elliott, my dilemma was always one of love. Did I allow Peter to die in front of a firing squad? Or did I fight and do a deal? Yes, I saved someone who had once been a traitor, but I'm sure I won't be the last. When all's said and done, what did the Lord put us on this earth to do, if not to love and be loved?

There! Now you have my story. I'll let you decide how it should end.

Yours

Elsie Sowerby

That evening, Elliott sat in his chair puffing away on his pipe while Ann read the letter. On finishing, she carefully folded it up and anxiously handed it back to her husband. He simply tossed it onto the fire stating, 'Well, as you said, there's never anything interesting in my mail.' Giving a playful wink, he slowly eased the pipe back into his mouth.

Ann just smiled and gently squeezed his hand.

~~~

</div>
~~~

Extra Bonus

The author has written a short epilogue to this book,
which is available as a free ebook download to members
of his readers group.

Join and get your copy here:

www.chrisbrookes.info/vipmailing list.html

———————————————

Books in the series

ENTANGLEMENT of FATE
An epic journey of destiny
inspired by the true story
of Walter …

ENTANGLEMENT of REVENGE
A pit disaster
A shocking secret
A motive as old as time

ENTANGLEMENT of DECEIT
Behind each face
lies a troubled
story …